Demons of London

by Michael E Bell

Published by Fleedleflump
1st Edition, July 2014
ISBN-10: 0992767539
ISBN-13: 978-0992767532

DEDICATION

These stories are dedicated to me ol' mate Dave. Without his love for the Mike Radshaw character, I'd never have written so many adventures.

CONTENTS

ACKNOWLEDGMENTS

Demons of London is the product of several years' writing, revising and feedback.

As ever, I owe an immeasurable debt to the peer reviewers on Fanstory.com. In particular (but no particular order):

Adewpearl

Hitcher

Smurphgirl

RaspE

Lindalcreel

Joy Graham

N K Wagner

Barbara.Wilkey

THE TALL TALE – PART 1

THE TALL TALE – PART 1

"There was no reason for optimism." I swiped my hand horizontally for emphasis. "The water was grim, the walls were closing in and my balls were so retracted, I could've coughed marbles. That's what nerves do for you. The guy with the basin haircut kept getting pulled under by some random tentacle, the cool bloke was more interested in shite one-liners than escape and the others were as much use as marshmallow underpants."

Our gazes met across air that shimmered from the immense heat billowing through it. Well, it was either heat or the recent blow to my head – hard to be sure. She blinked with what might have been eyelids and I took it as my cue to continue.

"Thanks for asking. Yes, indeed, some of them tried. The hairy fellow – you know, the one who sounds like bigfoot with his nuts caught in a zip – tried hitting the walls. Not the best plan in the world but I admired his enthusiasm. Someone tried bracing a pole made of tinfoil between the closing walls – should've known that wouldn't work, really."

Another blink, followed by a voice so guttural you could use it to define the word 'sepulchral' … and advertise cough medicine. "What about you, Radshaw – what did you do?"

I winked at her. "I pressed pause. Seriously, watching Star Wars is bad for my stress levels and I needed a break." The frown that slithered over her face could've killed a teenage boy band. "It was a good pause, though," I qualified. "You know – a real classic

VHS effort with bad expressions and inexplicably waving limbs."

A hand made of bunions, warts and spikes crunched into the table next to my head. "Do not fuck with me, Radshaw. You haven't the stamina."

"No offence, love," I swallowed the football-size lump of terror in my throat, "but I prefer my dates with guts on the inside and a singing voice slightly higher than Vin Diesel with flu."

She leaned in far enough to send rotting-meat breath into my mouth. "You are not special, Radshaw. You are not different." Her lips brushed mine, slick with slimy spittle, and then she turned to leave. "You will tell us what we want to know – I promise you."

I watched her demonic form stagger from the room, one foot clacking and the other squelching. Trust me when I say you don't want a description. Some great designer deity apparently decided all demon types should be scary ahead of practical and, though that made as much sense as a David Lynch film, it was undeniably effective.

My fingers flexed as I checked the bonds clamping me to the stone slab. Predictably, they were still strong and hadn't rotted conveniently since last time I tested them. The room they had me in was a cave dressed up to look like a hospital room – if hospitals used rugged slate beds and demonic nurses. Sourceless, luminescent light was spreading through the room like a visual pox, flickering and glaring in some places, pale and shy in others. A regular beep throbbed in the air but there was no machine to make it. If God was a teenage horror director, this would be his first set.

The deformed female (I think) demon was the third they'd sent to question me since I was caught in the lobby of a particularly foul-smelling realm. So far, I'd been able to handle it. I played the part of a nosey investigator who'd stumbled through the wrong door. Of course, they knew who I was – the same Mike Radshaw who kept pissing in their pool and living to tell the tale – but they were keeping me alive to find out why I was there. Ironically enough, that *was* why I was there.

It seemed the obvious approach but, so far, they hadn't tried torture.

"Long may that continue," I muttered.

"Perhaps we should try physical pain, Radshaw, hmm?" My new visitor strode into the dim room. He was a stereotype demon – humanoid with red skin, black teeth in a predator's smile, horns you could hang Thor's hammer from and claws like a giant cat. As subtle as a Michael Bay film, he nevertheless tied my guts up in knots. The oldest scary visuals are usually the best.

"Stay away from my furniture," I said. It was lame but all I could push out past the liquid panic sloshing in my stomach. He was naked, of course – custom built to make me feel physically inadequate – and muscles pulsed like writhing lovers beneath his skin as he slunk towards me.

He was at my bedside in moments, clawed hand curling round my wrist while the other stroked the length of a finger. I felt like Harrison Ford at the mercy of Rutger Hauer's simulant but there was nothing I could do about it. Instead of fighting, I matched his gaze, hoping the boldness in my eyes belied the weeping child within.

"What the fuck are you doing here, Radshaw?" he growled. I swear, a line of spittle crawled between those dark teeth and snaked down his chin while he spoke. You have to be one scary bastard to pull that off without looking like a prize idiot.

"An excellent question," I whispered.

He grinned. "This is no place for a human."

Remember why you're here, remember why you're here, remember why you're here. I swallowed. "Send in the bossman. I know you're not him – he'd have put some pants on. I'll only talk to the guy in charge."

I had time to hear his responding chuckle before the pain started. Do you know that feeling where you're not sure if you want to puke, piss yourself, or faint – preferably all at the same time? That's what I felt when his claw pushed down underneath my fingernail. A stab of warm agony thrust through my bones into my chest, dragging a cough from my throat and tears from my eyes. My face turned hotter than vindaloo diarrhoea and sweat blossomed like mould blisters across my forehead. I felt my legs jerking around and a grating sensation in my throat. It took a moment to realise I was screaming.

He pushed harder and I felt the flesh peeling from my finger. My bladder gave way as darkness infringed on my vision. If nothing else, unconsciousness would give me a break.

"Leave us." It was a small sound – thin and low to the ground. A child's voice with an underlying tone so adult it should be restricted to special shops in dark alleys. Footsteps retreated as the typically terrifying demon departed. I gasped in some breaths past my raw throat until the fog lifted. Refusing to look at my finger, I rested my eyes instead on my new tormentor, wondering what new levels of visual repugnance they were sending my way. I couldn't possibly have prepared myself.

A boy stood beside my bed. He was about eight years old, grinning through a face mask of freckles, and as ginger as Geri Halliwell in sepia. I shuddered as I spoke. "Next, you'll be telling me you're in charge around here."

His grin broadened. "Ten points for the silly human."

"Is that your age or a pube count?" I know, I know – winding up the demons was probably the stupidest idea since laptops without keyboards, but hey – sometimes stupid ideas work.

"I like you, Radshaw. You have no concept of caution or self-preservation. I find that entertaining."

"Yeah, it's like someone took Russell Brand and Jimmy Carr and rolled them up into a new Top Gear presenter. Are we finished with the mutual masturbation, or shall I take the piss out of you some more?" Blood was dripping from my ruptured finger – I could feel the tickle as it trickled across my hand. It was time to get on with this. "Seriously – who do I have to annoy to get some answers around here?"

"You've annoyed everyone you need to, believe me. My name is Belial, and this is my realm you've stumbled into."

I matched his gaze for several moments. "I've

heard of Belial. He's meant to be one serious motherfucker – the kind of demon heroes run from and sane men don't believe in. Nowhere in that legend is he described as a ten-year-old ginger minger called Ralph."

"My name is not Ralph."

"Well, it should be."

The freckled forehead creased into a frown. "You are an odd man, Radshaw. I can see why the others find you so frustrating. Now," he leaned across me, a red-tinted shadow, and all at once there was nothing funny about him. "Tell me what brought you here."

"Really?" I croaked. My mouth was as barren as Bin Laden's sense of humour. "At your age, I don't think you meet the certificate requirements for my story?"

"We age more slowly than you, Radshaw. I'm thousands of years old. Ours is a culture developed beyond reality, beyond morality, beyond the hopeless ken of man." He spat the last word. Perhaps I'd finally said something to upset him.

I mustered the shreds of my defiance – I needed him riled so I could hold his attention. "I've got more developed cultures between my toes."

The boyish nostrils flared and warm air tousled my eyebrows. His face filled the world. "Start talking, or I'll send the big guy back in, and this time he'll use *all* the tools at his disposal. What brought you here?"

I was particularly aware of my wet trousers as I stared into those demon eyes. There's a place past terror where everything's either hilarious or suicide-inducing. I've been there more times than I want to think about and now it feels like that old armchair everyone hoards in the spare room. I call it the 'fuck-it phase' — it's damned handy.

"Water," I whispered. "Get me some water. I have lots to say."

THE DOOR

THE DOOR

I pulled the trigger and the entire building erupted into flame and rubble. My blood-soaked hands lost their grip on the gun as I was hurled into the air, flailing like a rag doll. Hot fingers tore at my clothes and Lucifer cast a breath across my face. Then I slammed down on the roof of my car. Glass burst in glistening showers around me, the car alarm filled my ears with its cacophony, and through it all somebody screamed. It might have been me. Then the whole world blurred and faded to black.

*****

One hour earlier.

"He should have called the cops, Amy. This is a waste of my fucking time," I growled as I pulled in at the kerb. "I could've been heading up protection for a certain pop star at Wembley tonight; an evening spent walking behind a mighty fine arse. Instead, I have to put Steve on it so I can come and look at a fucking disused factory in a seriously shitty neighbourhood. This is *not* my idea of fun!"

My car stereo let out a short burst of static, indicating my assistant was laughing and covering her microphone so I wouldn't know. "Cool it, Mike. You know Mr Black only trusts you to do his bidding. Besides, he pays better than pop stars."

I took my seatbelt off. "I bet his arse is less fun to watch, though," I mumbled.

"What, boss?"

"Never mind. Listen, Amy, this place looks like it's not been used since the blitz, so sod knows why Mr Black's so bothered about it. The suspicious activity is probably just squatters or local drug dealers. All stuff for the cops to handle. I don't think this will take long."

"Gotcha, boss. Be careful, anyway. Mr Black gives me the creeps."

I smiled. "You watch too many Buffy re-runs, Amy. Everything gives you the creeps."

Another burst of static. "Boss, if I found Buffy scary I'd run a mile from you in the mornings. See you in a bit."

The line cut off before I could think up a witty retort, so with a sigh I grabbed my phone from its Bluetooth dock, got out of my car and headed round to the boot. Be careful, she'd said. If I was honest, the mysterious Mr Black gave me the creeps as well as Amy. He contacted us only by phone, and used a voice altering device to disguise his tones. What made him pick Mike's Celebrity Security to be his lapdogs was anyone's guess, as most of his work involved checking seemingly random properties for signs of break-in. The guy definitely had a mafia boss complex. It was a good thing he paid as well as he did.

"Fucking pretentious wanker," I said, strapping a pistol from the car boot into my shoulder holster. "You've got to stop talking to yourself, Mike, or you'll be in the loony bin before forty finds you."

I locked up the car and headed towards the disused building looming in front of me like the grim reaper. "Minus the scythe," I added vocally. I was in one of those weird quiet parts of inner city London that just seem like dead pockets; places of Victorian industry now long abandoned, seen only in passing from the trains that swooped back and forth on the raised rails above. A chain fence blocked my path, adorned with twin coils of S-wire and a plethora of notices warning me cameras, alarms and guard dogs would all be my undoing should I dare to enter unauthorised. The factory beyond was all dirty bricks, decaying wood-frame windows and a cracked courtyard with weeds invading through every orifice. Not the type of place to beckon burglars.

I dragged a loose corner of fence to one side with ease and slipped through into the factory grounds. I stamped a couple of times loudly, warning notices in mind, and looked around. Silence.

"All bark, no bite," I murmured as I headed for the nearest window.

No signs of movement betrayed intruders as I approached but the small, square panes of glass were so dirty and distorting, trolls could be having a party in there for all I knew. "A bloody quiet troll party, mind you."

A subtle sense of unease was creeping over me. I hoped it was just the nasty damp-infested walls and filth that were causing the tense, tight feeling in my gut, but hope's like water in a paper cup when all your instincts are shouting doom and gloom. I reached the window; still no movement, so I pinched my jacket cuff in one hand and used it to wipe a clean space to look through.

"Fuck. My. Arse."

The freshly cleaned glass went opaque again as

my breathing accelerated, but I knew what I'd seen. I backed away from the window, dragging my phone from my pocket, and pressed the speed-dial preset for Amy.

"Mike's Celebrity Security, how may I-"

"It's me, A. I need you to call the cops and send them over here, now. The bomb guys. S.O... whichever S.O. they are." I could feel the phone shaking against my ear. I hadn't seen that much fertiliser in one place since the eighties, back when I was a cop and the IRA were busy. Bags of the stuff filled the space inside, stacked floor to ceiling and, in front of that wall of death, a small table with some electronics and what I thought was a stick of Composition 4 plastic explosive, which would make an effective detonator.

"Bomb guys? Boss, what's going on there?"

I headed for the fence. "What's going on is I'm getting the fuck away from this place. This is either prep for the opening of London's biggest ever organic fruit and veg emporium, or someone's planning to piss on a hell of a lot of parades."

Amy's voice sounded shaky when she replied, "Okay, Mike. I'll call them now. You get out of there."

I killed the call as I reached the fence, but then a sound floated to me from the direction of the factory and my blood turned to icy pins in my veins. It was a baby's cry, frightened and thin, and in that moment my head turned to mush. I couldn't let a bomb go off in the middle of London, and I certainly couldn't let it vaporise a child.

"Bloody instincts!" I hissed, and jogged towards the warehouse door. When I reached it, the sense of unease from earlier turned into outright fear. The door looked ancient, hewn from a single hunk of solid oak, but had no visible lock or handle. From a distance it looked normal but, as I stood close to the timber, it seemed deeply unnatural. It emanated malevolence like a throbbing wound sends waves of pain and nausea through the body. I kicked it, and felt a little better, but it gave no sign of opening.

Looking to the side, I saw something even more bizarre. A section of wall next to the strange door was shimmering, as though viewed through waves of heat. "What the?"

I moved over to it, running a hand gingerly along the grime-caked bricks. When my fingers reached the shimmer, everything felt soft. My digits sunk to the first knuckle in a section of wall that felt like soft cheese. I flinched backward. A bead of sweat dribbled down the centre of my forehead and tickled my nose.

"Fuck this shit, Mike. Back off and wait for the cops."

I started to do as my voice advised but then it came again; that wailing, eerie call of a child in danger. "Ah, sod it! No guts, no grisly and meaningless death," I said, and walked straight into the wobbling wall.

As I hoped, there was little resistance, although the sensation of squeezing my face through rubbery dough almost made me puke. I took two tough steps, fighting as though walking against a gale, and then stumbled as the pressure vanished and I found myself...

Where?

"Where the hell am I?"

Far from a factory, I was in a dripping, cavernous tunnel. The walls, dark and slick, wheezed and shifted as though breathing and an accompanying breeze wafted against me rhythmically. My feet splashed in something that smelled of rotting fish. I turned around and there was the shimmering wall, looking identical to the other side. I pushed my hand back out through it, wanting to be sure I could go back that way.

"This place gets weirder by the minute. What in all that's stupid am I doing here?" I sighed. "You're saving a kid, Mike. That's what you're doing. Although, what the fuck a baby's doing in this place is beyond me. Here goes nothing."

I headed into the tunnel, which seemed to be angling vaguely downward into darkness. I jogged for what seemed like ages, gun in hand. For all I knew, the weapon was completely useless here, but it made me feel manly and stopped me from running back to my car wailing. Occasionally, a cry would drift to my ears, egging me on, but I was starting to get anxious. If the bomb guys turned up and tripped the device, I'd be too dead to know about it.

The tunnel narrowed sharply and turned ahead. I sneaked towards the blind corner, flinching slightly as the wall swelled and pressed against me like a sweating, damp, amorous sponge. A new noise was audible; a wet clicking that put me in mind of knitting needles soaked in blood. I gently squeezed the safety on my gun into the off position, closing my eyes and searching for some courage to combat the wall of terror in front of me. I was right at the corner now. I'd come this far. "Get on with it, you pussy!" I said beneath my breath, and flicked my head briefly round the corner.

Images burned into my mind's eye, recorded in horror during my momentary glance. A circular chamber with another tunnel opening on the opposite side, and in the centre of the floor a butcher's block, dripping gore. A heaving, misshapen beast the colour of blood with claws for fingers and a head made entirely of fangs. Needles threaded with something stretchy and organic, like sinew. A baby's form, dissected and re-assembled in a grotesque likeness of the creature standing over it. All accompanied by the sound of talons, tapping together as if playing percussion to a tune. My stomach felt like it was trying to burst from my mouth.

I hadn't made the conscious effort but my finger curled round the trigger of my trusty gun. Well, I say trusty but in reality this would be its first outing. Celebrity protection is all about intimidation and bluster. If some sick bastard calls your bluff and violence happens, you're as screwed as a rubber drill bit. I felt the cool sliver of the trigger shaking against the meat of my finger, then admitted it wasn't the gun shaking.

Forty nine percent of me was running for the exit with piss running down my legs, but fifty one percent propelled me round that corner, screaming as I went. I shot bullets into the demon thing until the chamber clicked empty, and continued to press the trigger repeatedly. It flew backwards against a soft wall, black blood spurting from it where my shots landed, and collapsed to its face. Dark ichor continued to ooze from its wounds but it didn't move as I stood over it, clicking gun aimed down.

Black juice pulsed and spread like an oil slick across skin too smooth to be natural. The very sight of its dead form pressed gall into my throat and forced a harsh wheeze into my breaths. I looked at my hand, pulling its trigger like a movie character after his first, intense kill.

"Stop it, Mike. Stop it, it's done, it's dead. You rock." I almost giggled, and then stopped myself. Before anything else, I loaded a fresh clip into my gun. Then, satisfied the demon (what else was I going to call it?) was dead, I turned to the tiny form on the butcher's block, and tears flooded my eyes. I've seen some sick shit in my life, and I thought nothing could shock me, but the sight of that tiny, vulnerable human form, cut up and re-arranged for some unimaginable purpose, almost unmanned me.

At that point, I had to know why. I might have failed to save the little mite, but I could get to the bottom of this. I headed for the other tunnel. I knew my eyes must be as wide as saucers and, truth be told, I didn't know if any of this was real. I guess there's a limit to how many insane things the mind can see before disbelief becomes numb acceptance. "I don't care what world I'm in, I'm not having this."

The other tunnel stayed tight all the way, occasionally caressing my hair as its flexible ceiling bulged close. I walked for a few minutes before a shuffling sound came to me and I slowed my pace, gun at the ready. It sounded like sand paper, that was all I could think of; sand paper being rubbed rhythmically on soft timber. Then I crept upon a scene of stunning chaos.

The chamber was so large, I could see no other walls or ceiling. It was lit by flaming torches set out in a regular grid on the floor. I stood in the tunnel mouth, raised slightly above the cavern floor. Before me stood a line of the demon creatures, their backs to me, and walking in symmetrical lines before them were hundreds, perhaps thousands, of mutilated people. They shuffled with a zombie-like trudge, perfectly in unison, a repulsive army of the grotesque. Each one was re-arranged like the baby, internal parts now stapled to the outside, limbs attached in a hideous representation of a demon. They should not have been able to walk, but they managed it.

"Jesus in a whorehouse," I whispered. Blasphemy felt somehow appropriate right then. A part of me knew I had to get out, to warn people, but what was I going to say? 'Hello, police? I just stumbled across some demons cutting people up and turning them into deformed, zombie warriors. I think they're building an army. Yes, I'd like pink highlights in my padded cell, and I take an XXL straight jacket, thank you.'

No, I had to do something about this myself. An idea struck me so hard that I was worried a glowing light bulb might appear above my head. I turned and headed for the surface at a hurried creep. I had to set off that bomb!

When I reached the smaller chamber, I made to skirt the butcher's block. I had no wish to see the mutilated baby again. I stepped over the dead demon in its sticky, tar-like puddle of blood and was almost across to the other side when a tiny whimper sounded and my breath caught in my throat. I turned towards the block to see the baby wriggling. Transfixed, I walked over to it, and promptly doubled over, hurling my lunch onto the floor.

I'd thought the little thing dead, but clearly whatever process it underwent was completed because the poor thing was now awake and moving. It wriggled and cried, turning a head that was a mass of gristle from side to side. Then a maw affixed to one temple, complete with messily inserted teeth and a single eye, fixed on me. An eerie howl pierced the air and an arm with the bone protruding from its stump pointed at me. The faint shuffling from below stopped.

As innocent as I wanted it to be, I knew the tiny demon just warned those below of my presence. It was like the most grotesque intruder alarm imaginable, and I needed to get out of there.

Vomit dribbling from my lips, consciousness shrunk back in madness and disgust, I raised my gun over my head. "For fuck's sake," I said. Then I brought the gun butt slamming down on the demon baby's head, mashing it to a pulp against the butcher's block. I prayed for the first time in my life; that I had acted quickly enough and avoided raising any alarm.

I turned and fled, fixing my mind on one thought, the only one I knew mattered; detonate that bomb!

As the breathing tunnel widened I heard a roar of inhuman anger behind me and increased my pace. Right then, I would have sworn I could break every running record in the Olympics, I ran so damned fast. As the shimmering wall appeared ahead of me, I threw a glance over my shoulder. A demon was hot on my heels, its teeth and claws glinting at the edge of the gloom behind.

Without hesitation, I hurled myself into the soft wall and burst into London's early evening grey. I could hear two-tones in the distance. That would be the bomb cops. I almost laughed. How long had I been down there? It didn't matter. I staggered across the weedy concrete towards the fence, turning to check my position against the window. How much distance did I need? That was probably irrelevant, given the amount of explosive I'd seen. I reached the fence and fell through the loose panel, then pulled myself to my feet and aimed my gun through the window. There it was; the vague shape of that detonator on the table. I knew I was a good enough shot.

Tyres screamed behind me and the wind flapped my jacket. From the shimmering portal next the strange door, I saw a head formed entirely of teeth emerge.

"Drop it!" yelled a voice. "Armed police!"

I smirked. "Fuck 'em if they can't take a joke," I said, and pulled the trigger.

*****

The next voice I heard was Amy's, and I woke to see her face framed by a grubby hospital ceiling.

"Mike!" she said, "thank God, you're awake!"

I groaned. "My head feels like an elephant took a dump in it." Memories flooded back in an unwelcome rush. I strained my head up towards her. "Am I in much trouble?"

Amy didn't seem to know whether to grin or frown. "You were, yeah. But then the police arrested some guys for making the bomb that went off. Apparently they're all in some cult which claims to be a secret order of church knights, working for the Vatican. They're taking the rap for everything."

My head slumped back on the pillow and I sighed. "Fuck a doodle-do."

"What the hell happened, boss?" she asked, but something must have shown in my face because she shook her head immediately. "Never mind, you can tell me later."

"How long's it been?"

She smiled. "You've been unconscious nearly a week, Mike. We really didn't know if you'd make it."

Another face loomed into view; Steve's concerned countenance. "You're one tough bastard, boss," he said. Then he laughed. "Like in that film."

I grinned. "I've only got one thing to say to you, Steve, you lucky git."

"What's that?"

"Next time, I'm taking the pop star's arse, and Mr Black can damned well kiss mine!"

MICHAEL E BELL

NUTS

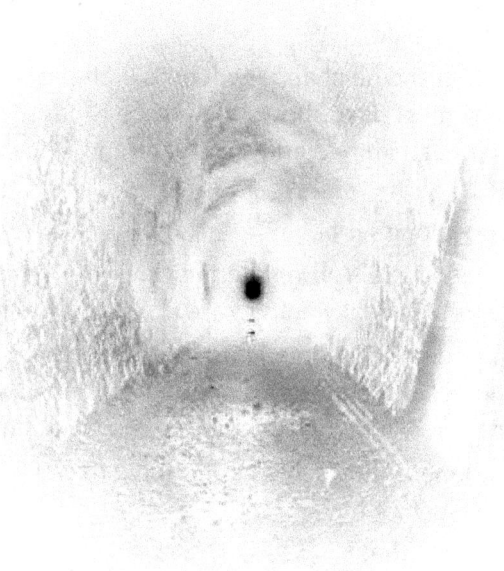

NUTS

The door was closed. In the distance, I heard concussive crashes as breaching charges detonated like mini bombs. The firearms teams were going in, and here I was looking at the rear entrance like a confused boy scout in the bushes at a gay pride rally. I apologised internally for the thought which may have offended any nearby telepaths. Then I summoned up all my anger at what these sick wankers had done, all the urgency and bile that tore through my system, and I booted that bastard door with everything I had.

The shock reverberated up my leg, stabbing into my knee like a bullet's kiss. I gritted my teeth against it, smiling grimly through the pain as the door twisted and the frame shook. It didn't open, but it was mostly destroyed; nothing a solid shoulder couldn't finish off. I backed up, taking a lung-full of cold, pre-dawn London air and shaking my arms out to the sides.

A train passed behind and above me with a gentle *chuggadagung ... chuggadagung.* Gulls yarked as they floated above the Thames. The dirty concrete was solid beneath my feet, its weeds grasping at my Doc Martens. In front of me, the near-dead wooden door rocked, offering repeating glimpses of a dark interior. I held my gun in both hands down at one side.

The gang members were all meant to be at the front of the factory, where SO19 were busy doing their SWAT impression. I was at the back door, ostensibly guarding, but there was no way the firearms squad was getting all the glory on this one. I readied my shoulder, swung back on my heels, and launched myself forward.

The building was ostensibly a chocolate bar factory; one of London's oldest. I even liked the bar they produced, with its sweet nut-packed mushy innards. Why they'd changed the name from a noble long-distance run to a word resembling ladies' underwear was beyond me, but who am I to argue with confectionary manufacturers?

My shoulder took the door with all my weight behind it. As I'd hoped, my shoulder won, and suddenly I was careening through a dingy storeroom, swinging my gun up as I staggered. Never look anywhere your gun isn't pointed; that's what the training said. No, hang on a minute, I think that was Stephen Seagal, but it's good advice nevertheless. As my eyes adjusted to the interior gloom, I pressed myself against a wall and span from one side to the other in a 180 degree arc, taking in the world along the short barrel of my pistol. I had no chance to gather my thoughts before there was a blinding flash; muzzle flash, I realised as I saw the gang member who'd fired at me lit up like an angel talking to mortals through a diffuse glow. Well, assuming there's an angel with an 'I Fucked ur Granny n She Loved it' tattoo knocking around somewhere. The point is, he'd shot at me, and as far as I could tell he was dead on target.

*****

The name's Mike Radshaw. I was a detective for the Metropolitan Police for a long time, doing my best to catch the worst elements of society with little to no funding at my disposal. I spent a while as a private security contractor, but a bomb in a warehouse changed my perspectives a little on that. Now I'm a private investigator, available to take on all the shit cases nobody else wants. Usually that means contracting to the cops, such as this deal to track down a particularly nasty gang. Yep, you could say my career has come full circle, but I've seen lots, from the grotesque through the mad to the just plain bonkers, and that's better preparation than most have for facing the things I get into.

Anyway, back to the present, I guess. I bashed my way through the back door into that gang headquarters; mistake!

*****

A subsonic round would get to me after the firing sound, but this guy didn't look like the subsonic type so I'd have a hole in me before I got any audio warning. It's a funny feeling, being in that moment you're sure is your last. It's as though time stops for you briefly, just long enough for realisation to dawn like a wave of bile rolling across your landscape. You have a moment for regrets and triumphs, even time to think about how the guy who fired the bullet has angel attributes. Of course, you've not got time to actually DO anything about it; that's just one of the sub-clauses in the ineffable laws of reality.

In any world but my own strange, little esoteric one, I shouldered through a door, brought my gun up, and a guy shot me. His bullet split my right cheek and crashed through the packing crates stacked behind me.

Pain speared into the back of my head as splinters invaded, and those caused me to flinch more than my flapping cheek. A small part of my head - the handy bit that still worked while the rest was yelling 'ohfuckohfuckohfuck' - told me to hurl myself sideways. I did so, tripping and falling to the floor. I probably looked about as elegant as an elephant ballerina but the move did save my life. The guy whose tattoo had apparently pleasured my granny fired again, violently perforating the air I'd recently occupied.

That small part of my head raised my gun, squinted to be sure of its aim, and pulled the trigger. Granny-fucker's nose disappeared into his skull and he flew backwards through a doorway.

I blew a gust of air through near-closed lips in relief, then almost fainted from the pain when my cheek rasped. I put a hand to the wound and wished I hadn't. Deciding it would have to wait, I climbed to my feet, keeping my gun pointed at Granny-fucker's feet. I'd made enough noise to conjure an army of the dead - oh please, shit no, let this gang not be another bunch of weird demons or zombies! Company could arrive at any moment, and not the kind you invite in for tea and games.

I staggered to the door my target fell through. He was dead, alright, and even if he was a donor, the nose would be no use.

I shook my head to clear the adrenalin-induced nutty cobweb thoughts.

"Very fucking professional, Mike!" I muttered to myself. "Make more noise than Brian Blessed with Tourette's Syndrome, kill a guy with his own nose, and get shot to boot. SO19 are gonna have your bollocks for breakfast!"

I thought about my psychiatrist, a man I'd been leaning on more than I wanted to since an unfortunate demon-baby-exploding-building incident. He'd almost managed to stop me talking to myself, although I'd pointed out to him that I did that long before I was given flying lessons by a mountain of fertiliser. He'd also admonished me about judging situations based purely on my instincts, but I was still working on that one.

"My door is always open," he kept saying. I made a small note to take advantage of that when I got out of my current predicament. Feet were smacking ground nearby and, slightly more muffled, gunshots cracked and split the air. This was a big building, and the trained cops with the decent artillery were the other side of the violent gang we'd come to apprehend. A sensible version of me would have retreated through the broken door, called for assistance, and faced the gang members in single file as they emerged.

Somewhere inside, that guy exists, but I've never met him. I pushed on, heading through a short corridor to the bottom of a stairwell. It smelled like a council tower block, like some chavs'd had a pissing party, but I tried to block it out. A door ahead led to the main gunfight, so I headed up the pale concrete steps.

These guys were your standard, run-of-the-mill, drug dealing, pointless wastes of air. They'd distinguished themselves, however, with their fundraising side-lines. In my investigations of their activities I'd stumbled on a dark web link that took me to some decidedly uncomfortable images. The dealers had uncovered a rich vein of gold whilst mining the depths of kiddie porn. There is, it seems, always a rich businessman just looking for a shocking vice to pursue. That the gang producing the photos and vid clips had no interest in their own material made it somehow worse. I mean, who tortures children to pay for drugs transactions? That's like amputating a leg to cure an itchy toe.

As I crested a landing I was met with a vision of urban office hell. Walls so thin you could have printed the paint onto them sprawled out like a magnolia army before me. Doors were dotted around, filled with that bobbly glass that makes people look like cellulite monsters. Desks stood their ground like machine gun nests, unmanned and sad. Everybody must be downstairs taking pot-shots at policemen. That suited me just fine; I was here for evidence, and the sickening throb in my cheek made me hope my pursuers wouldn't look for me up here.

A sound caught my attention, from an office off to one side. I hugged the wall like it was my bodyguard, inwardly acknowledging that it'd be less use than a tissue condom for halting bullets. Sidling up to the open door emitting sounds, I took a deep breath and a lightning-quick peek inside.

There were two of them, dressed in eighties throwbacks and garish headscarves. Two white men - no, scratch that; if these guys had pubes, they were newcomers - two white boys. One sat on a ragged old sofa whilst the other hammered feverishly on a keyboard before a blinking screen. Neither of them saw me.

"Whatchoo doin' after this, man?" said the sitting one.

"Yo, I's gettin' laid tonight, man," said MC Keyboard-Hammer.

"Go, boy! Who you shaggin'?"

Tap tap, taptaptap, "one sec, bro. I gotta run these clean-up scripts or I'll be gang-meat, man."

"Don' be avoiding the question, innit! Tell me."

A sigh. "It's Laura, man. Yo, don't laugh, she alright from behind."

"She is mingin', mate," came a reply interspersed with cackles. "She's a total munter."

"Yeah boy, but she 'as got a wazza set of jugs, innit."

Whiteboy jive, I thought to myself, wincing. These guys were so far out of their depths, their soles must be burning. I strode into the room, gun held confidently in their direction. "Go home, boys. Head back to Mummy, if she'll take you. You got ten seconds before I decide you're actually the gangsters you like to think you are. After that, I'll just arrest or shoot you, depending on my mood."

MC Keyboard-Hammer turn to face me, his eyes wide beneath the badly wrapped black bandana. "Yo cous, you got no clue who you fuckin' wiv, man."

The other, slouched on the tatty sofa, put a hand behind his back. "You crazy, maan, we gonna smoke you like a mu'fucker."

I didn't wait to see what kind of toy he had ready. I pulled the trigger and killed the cushion next to his head, showering him in hot foam fragments. "Grow up!" I roared, "and *fuck off*!"

They scampered past me then, heading for the door I'd entered through. Judging by their expressions, their Mums would be doing some emergency laundry when they got home.

I headed for the computer. The little scrote had been writing a script on screen. I know as much about computer programming as a blond from Essex knows about calculus, but I could decipher enough to see which directories the code was intended to delete. I closed the window without running the script, dug my USB memory stick from my pocket, and set the dodgy files copying onto it.

Having alternately told me the process would take ten seconds and three days, the computer settled on twelve minutes.

"Marvellous," I muttered, and cocked my gun. That was twelve minutes longer than I wanted to spend here.

I heard running footsteps outside the door and brought my gun up just as a huge dude in Bermuda shorts and a string vest hove into view. In the time it took me to recover from the hideous print his trousers sported he'd managed to fire his shotgun at me. I pulled my trigger just as something way too hard and heavy pounded into my stomach. Bermuda guy's foot exploded and I was hurled backwards into the tatty sofa, which promptly tipped over and deposited me on the floor behind it.

I clutched my gut and groaned. Sod knew where my gun had gone; it'd been flung from my hand when I did my flying impression. The guy was roaring in pain but the roars were getting closer. I tried to move but my stomach felt like it'd been used as a trampoline by an ambitious blue whale.

A foot with a hole in it and blood squelching with each step appeared round the end of the upturned sofa. Above it was one seriously pissed gangster with tears on his face and a shotgun clutched before him. He worked the pump and levelled the barrel at my face.

"Beanbags, motherfucker!" he shouted.

That's a new one, I thought. Then he fired.

*****

A thought was trying to get my attention but it was like a midget waving its arms in a crowd of giants. If those bastards would just stop playing war drums, perhaps a guy would be able to think. I hadn't felt like this since the time I drank a whole crate of Diamond White and woke up in a tranny bar in Soho wearing just my tie and a Tesco carrier bag. Damned stag parties ... damned idiots getting married!

I'd only known her six months, and the marriage turned out even shorter.

That insistent thought slapped my face and told me to snap out of it but only succeeded in amplifying the pain. I vowed that, should I ever meet the evil git who invented drums, I'd shoot him on the spot.

"Yo, he comin' round," said a voice.

"MC Keyboard-Hammer?" I murmured.

"Fuck you talkin' 'bout, man?"

My heart sank as reality made an unwanted

incursion into my awareness. That was not the voice of a pubeless wannabe. More like the voice of an evil arch-villain, or the bloke that does film trailer voiceovers. The nagging thought finally got through. 'Escape!' it shouted.

"Thanks," I replied aloud, "but you're a bit late."

"Yo, I think you scrambled his mayonnaise brain, man. He lookin' like Frankenstein's monster."

Another disembodied voice answered, this time in a tone I recognised with a gasping undercurrent of pain. "I don' give a shit. This mutha fucked up my foot."

"We need him to talk, man. Whatchoo thinkin, shootin' him with a beanbag slug at short range?"

The other guy sounded mighty pissed. "I was thinkin' that this mutha FUCKED UP MY FOOT!"

Great; not only had I been captured, I'd been captured by violent bastards who argued like an old married couple. The pain in my head throbbed with a vengeance and I laughed. "You two should get counselling," I said. Then I groaned as another gale of agony buffeted my brain. Why does laughter amplify any pain you happen to be experiencing? That's just not fair.

I decided to risk opening my eyes and was treated to the sight of an incoming fist. Stars exploded across my vision in a beautiful and complex display but I was too busy roaring in pain to properly appreciate it.

"Yo man, get the fuck outta here," shouted Film-Trailer-Voice. "You gonna kill this pussy whiteboy. Let me do this, man. Go fix your fuckin' foot or somethin'."

"He's mine when you finished, blud," spat Holy Foot. I cracked an eye open to see him limping away. I was left with FTV, a guy who looked like a rugby star crossed with a nightclub bouncer. There was tension in every bulging muscle and I could see steroids in the whites of his eyes and the distinct lack of bulge in his pants. He had on a string vest top and it didn't look funny; that's how hardcore scary this bloke was. He combined it with denim shorts and a number one head shave. If I was Mr T with a death wish, I'd have told him he looked rather camp.

I'm not Mr T, though, even though my thoughts were now pushing me to shout 'I ain't gettin' no plane, you crazy foo', and fetch me some milk!'. I like to think I know a hysterical thought when I formulate one.

Instead, I gazed on into his wide, scary eyes and said, "yes, Sir? What would you like to know?"

*****

We were in a basement that put me in mind of serial killers and Saw films. It was dark, dank, dingy, and all sorts of other yucky words starting with 'd'. All it needed was some chains hanging from the ceiling, clanking ominously as they swayed for no reason, and a sinister drip.

"You really fucked this up for us, man," said FTV. "We almost done here, an' you had ta bring the fuzz down on us."

I sighed as I winced and attempted thought through my swollen brain. "I assume you need me, or I'd be dead. So what did I fuck up? Your latest kiddie-fiddling video, a drug deal? I hope you're not expecting sympathy."

"Man, you don' know shit. We on our last day here, mission accomplished an' all that shit. We broke through down below, found us the door we lookin' for. The boss gonna be happy, but we gotta finish the job an' between you an' the fuzz, we got no guinea pigs left."

I looked into his wide eyes and mined the bitter anger in my gut to give myself courage. "You fucked children just to make money, arsehole. I don't care about any pissing door, or any shitty sob story you got to tell me. I ain't helping you."

The huge guy's face screwed up and I swear a tear escaped one eye before he turned away, wiping a meaty hand across his face.

"We didn' wanna do that, man," he said quietly. "That shit's hardcore fucked up. But the boss, he make the rules. We gotta get that door open, man. Drugs, bitches ..." he sniffed loudly, "an' kids. We sell whatever we gotta to pay for the guys we need." He turned back and pushed his face into mine. "All the sick shit I done, there ain't no way I'm gonna fail now. I'm already headed ta hell, whiteboy. May as well get paid."

There was no give in his face, so I swallowed and nodded. "So what do you need from me?"

A smile crawled across FTV's face and it wasn't entirely sane. "We foun' the door, man. You gonna open it."

*****

The door was closed, and by that I mean it looked permanently shut, like it was almost part of the wall around it. Hewn from what looked like ancient oak, it had harsh, alien words scrawled all over it. A little part of me wondered if it said 'Jeff woz ere' in ancient Aramaic or something. If it did say that, though, Jeff must have been the scariest motherfucker who ever lived, because just the sight of his writing made me want to piss my boxers.

We were at the end of a hollowed out tunnel, roughly cut by amateurs, and I wasn't at all sure the ceiling was trustworthy. The only light was cast by the torch FTV was carrying, and it had me sensing evil in every shadow. The writing on the door looked like hundreds of dead spiders, as though they'd given their lives to imprint a message of hate, fear, or foreboding. I was torn between wishing I could read it and clutching fervently to my ignorance.

A hand shoved my lower back and I stumbled closer to the horrid facade. "Fuckin' open it," said FTV.

From my closer perspective, I could make out a strange shimmer across the surface of the door, looking like heat in the distance. A cold thrill chased an ant colony up and down my back as I realised I recognised the phenomenon.

"This employer of yours," I whispered. "This boss you mention. Does he by any chance refer to himself as 'Mr Black'?"

The silence from behind me was all the confirmation I needed. I steeled myself against what was coming and pushed my hand forward carefully. As I'd thought, it pressed into the door as though it was made from marshmallow. My fingers quested through to the other side and it felt cold, oh so horribly cold. I quested further, pushing an entire hand through to the other side, into that terrifying other place I'd visited once before. Just as I was about to stop, my fingers touched something cold and solid. It flinched away from me and I swear I did a little crap right there on the spot.

There was sudden, harsh pain and I yanked my hand back through to see two of my fingers flayed open, blood rushing across my palm.

"Aaaaah!" I shouted, my mind filling with images of demons, teeth, and malformed babies with their bones sticking from their arms. Explosions filled my mind's eye, the sensation of being chased, running faster than my muscles were able to, being thrown through the air, smashing into the roof of my car.

"Yo, what the fuck you doin'? Open the fuckin' door, man!"

I turned and stared at FTV, my thoughts tumbling like a washing machine on spin. Something in my face must have scared him because he visibly shrank back. "I shit my pants!" I shouted at him, holding my split fingers before his face and shaking them. "I shit myself, you motherfucker!"

"Man, what the fuck?"

I grabbed him and span us round, pushing him towards the evil door. "You open it!" I spat into his face and his eyes opened even wider.

"Fuck you, man, why you think we got you? I ain't goin' in there!" For all his defiance he wasn't fighting me. Whatever expression I had on my face, it was doing a serious number on him.

Mr T blossomed to life in my head; clearly he was prominent in my subconscious at the moment. I leaned back, raised a leg, and planted my foot firmly in FTV's chest. "Get some nuts!" I shouted as he disappeared, screaming, through the door.

I turned and ran for it, trying to ignore the squelching in my underwear. If I got out of this alive, a bit of crap in my trousers was a price I was prepared to pay. As I passed each inexpertly placed shore, I kicked it out. My head was almost permanently turned backwards, too many memories of being chased by demons bashing through my awareness for me to look ahead. I kept that evil door in sight until a curtain of earth obscured it. Then I faced forward and ran like buggery. I felt like Indiana Jones, racing ahead of a giant boulder, except if he'd pooped himself then George Lucas sure as hell didn't reveal it in the theatrical release.

The whole world became a dirty, choking blur as I ascended into the basement, then to the ground floor, and finally out through the broken door I'd used to make my entry. I think I was sobbing when I finally collapsed on the concrete and concerned hands grabbed at me. I didn't care, though. I'd got out. I'd escaped again. It seemed Mr Black was forever likely to haunt me. I vowed as I lay there being tended to. I made a promise to myself that I'd get to the bottom of these doors and that manipulative bastard if I had to spend the rest of my life doing it.

"Don't be afraid, Mike," I muttered to myself. "You're a warrior." Then I blacked out.

*****

It was two days later that, having finally been released from hospital with a thoroughly bandaged hand and patched-up cheek, I finally mounted the steps to my psychiatrist's office. I wanted to tell him everything, from my experiences in the peanut chocolate bar factory to my plans to track down the enigmatic Mr Black. I needed his approval, his ratification. I would take advantage of his promise. I walked through the waiting area, turned down a corridor that would take me to his office, and stopped. My knees found the carpet as my consciousness shrank away.

I cackled like a hyena on laughing gas.

The door was closed.

A FLUTTER OF DEMONS

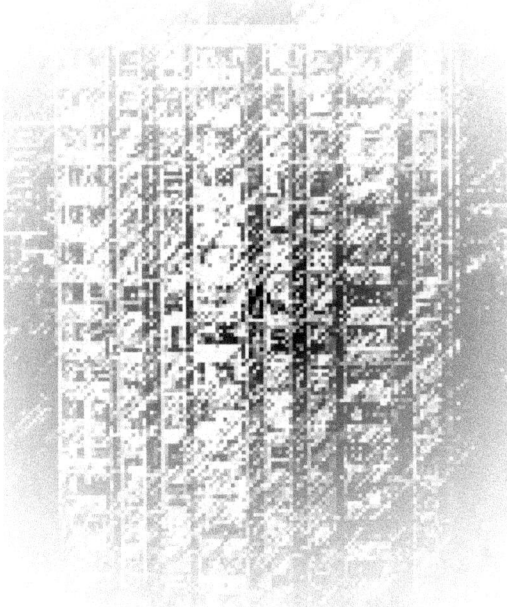

A FLUTTER OF DEMONS

The bumper whirled from the collision like a helicopter blade with wrathful intent and crashed through my windscreen. The world became a thick morass of twinkling shards, panic and pain. I yanked on the steering wheel as my bladder turned to ice and lead, sending my hired Ford Focus careening sideways, skidding and jerking like an animal fleeing a predator. Ahead, the visual cacophony of ruptured vehicles, smoke and debris was a blur I couldn't tear my gaze from. I turned my head to keep my eyes fixed on the destruction - through my sundered front window, then the side running towards the back. Closer and closer, it came - a terrible, undeniable end. I had just enough time to spot my client's Smart car - a crumpled, hopelessly misshapen mess in the middle of a scrap mountain - before I slammed backwards into the central partition of the M1 and screamed my way into unconsciousness.

*****

"Mike?" said a voice.

"Any response?" said another.

"Hmm?" I groaned. The first voice sounded vaguely familiar.

"Mike? Can you hear me?"

Unconsciousness peeled away like layers from an onion, leaving a core of unwelcome awareness in its wake. The voice belonged to Amy - my assistant. She might have been an angel, opening the door to my head with light shining around her, except I didn't like what she was illuminating. If this was a hangover, it was the kind that makes you eat dust all night and comes with a side order of pure self-loathing.

I debated opening my eyes but decided against it. "My throat feels like aliens gave me an anal probe and used the long version - you know, the one that extracts your tonsils from the inside."

"He may be delusional - possible concussion," said the unfamiliar voice.

"No," said Amy, sighing, "that's just his idea of humour."

Memories crept back into my head in loose fragments like dough being pushed through a sieve. I gathered them together and kneaded with mental knuckles until sense emerged. "What happened to Miss Guvern - did she survive?" My voice sounded like a rock whispering but at least it worked.

Amy's extended pause told me the news wasn't good. "She's alive," was her eventual response. "I don't think she'll be able to talk to you for a while, though - she's in a medically induced coma."

"What about me - how badly was I injured?"

She tutted. "You could open your eyes and look for yourself, you know."

"What if I've got no legs and I'm just a torso with my spine and bits hanging out, plugged into a computer so the government can speak to my consciousness and find out what happened before I died?"

"I'm not going to dignify that with a serious response. And no, you're not as handsome as Jake

Gyllenhaal - not even close."

I sighed and opened crusty eyes to see a depressingly dull hospital room around me. "You couldn't stroke your boss's ego, even when he's in terrible pain?"

"If you ever ask me to stroke anything, I'll be out of your life faster than a cheap curry. Really, you got off light, boss. You have a nasty gash on your arm from a bumper that went through your windscreen, but other than that, you just got yanked about." She blinked at me through fashionable glasses, her green eyes warmer than the tone she was taking. Her suit told me she was having a serious day but the bright red blouse beneath meant she had plans for later. Amy had a square jaw, if truth be told, but it was gracefully realised in a sweeping, delicate bone structure. Still, it was her loyalty and dependability I most valued. When your assistant's come to see you in hospital as often as she had me, you know they're a keeper. Her arm came forward with a cup of water and I choked down a few mouthfuls.

"That accident was no accident," I said while she wiped my chin.

"Are you still joking, or did you actually intend that sentence for human consumption?"

I blinked. "Help me up, Amy. I need to see her."

I was limping as we traversed the inexplicably huge distance from my bed to my client's, but I felt almost normal. My arm ached and bruises blossomed across my skin but my biggest problem was a massive pain in my arse. Either my muscles played a joke on me in the crash, or that alien probe joke wasn't as funny as I thought it was. I said as much to my trusty sidekick and she gave me a look like I was about to ask her to massage it better.

It can be really depressing when someone knows you so well.

We were stopped at the doors to the Intensive Therapy Unit by a security guard so big, it was a wonder he didn't project his own gravity field. I could see my client in her bed on one side, looking like a bleached mummy, various limbs held in apparatus. I only knew it was Miss Guvern because of the shock of pure white hair erupting from the top of the bandages. Even out of traction, the woman looked like Helena Bonham Carter after the fright of her life - a description more ironic than it first seemed.

A doctor was heading towards us so we waited until he exited.

"Are you Mike Radshaw?" asked the man before I could open my mouth. I squinted at him carefully for a few moments. I was *pretty* sure he wasn't somebody I'd pissed off in the past, but it was difficult to be certain.

"Errr, yes," I said. "How's Miss Guvern?"

"What relation to her are you?"

"I'm her dick."

He arched an eyebrow and I fought back a Roger Moore comment. Sighing, Amy explained to him that I meant 'detective' and the patient was my client.

The doctor nodded. "She was raving when she came in, shouting your name and that you needed to know something. Poor woman could barely breathe but she was determined."

Something tightened my chest. "What did she say?"

"She said 'the pitter-patter. Tell Radshaw it was the pitter-patter.' Over and over again. It was all we could do to calm her down. I don't know what the pitter-patter is, Radshaw, but it sure seemed important to her."

*****

I strode along Tottenham Court Road with a mission. London at night's like an LED rain forest these days. Neon's not such a thing anymore - those lingering shots of glowing concrete jungle from Michael Mann films don't hold so true. Now it's all piercing colours and bafflement. My name's Mike Radshaw and 'baffled' is my near-constant state of mind these days. I used to be a cop in the Met police, but one too many bonkers experiences left me with a burning desire for a quieter life. Like a total numpty, I sought that as a PI. As I might have guessed, the insane cases followed me.

My destination was a pub down a back-road with terrible decor and a worse reputation. The sign loomed from the shadows as I approached - a baby goat being serenaded by a violin player. Despite being innocent (ish), The Kid n Fiddler fell into disrepute thanks to unwelcome connotations. The landlord tried to change the name, only to be told it was five hundred years old and protected by heritage law. Nowadays, it served the cheapest beer in London for the highest prices and played host to a plethora of shady businesses.

The door creaked like a hundred arthritic knees as

I entered. It was three in the morning - way past closing time, but the authorities left this place alone. I bought a pint I had no intention of drinking from a barman so bored he could've been dead and sat in a very specific booth at the darkest extent of the common room. The Kid n Fiddler wasn't a place I enjoyed visiting but, ever since the case I'd worked in an abandoned factory, it'd been a rare source of helpful information. I encountered demons for the first time that day - literal as well as figurative. I destroyed a building to block an army of perverted babies and crushed a newborn's head with my gun.

Suffice to say, it was an unpleasant experience.

Since then, I've grown up fast. Demons are always there, trying to break through and wreak havoc. Lots of people know about this, but most of them are about as together as a handful of sand or so weird, Stanley Kubrick could use them for a character piece. Still, some voices are worth heeding. One of those was The Bloke Down The Pub - self-named. When people say of obscure information 'the bloke down the pub told me,' they're referring to this guy. As it turns out, he lives here, in this unfortunately named watering hole. Well, I say 'he' ...

"Radshaw. Always a pleasure." The voice came from my own mouth, vibrating my vocal chords like strings on a double bass. I resisted a powerful urge to wet myself.

"How do you do that with my voice? There are times I'd kill to be able to talk with that much malice."

"You lack the will."

I coughed and went to take a mouthful of my

drink, then thought better of it. Best to keep this conversation to the point or I'd end up unable to speak. "What's the pitter-patter?"

My nose snorted. **"A whimsical use of onomatopoeia."**

"I'm serious."

"You don't want to know, Radshaw. Leave this one alone."

I sighed and pinched the bridge of my nose. "I can't. There's a lady in hospital and I promised I'd help. Someone took out a whole swathe of the M1 to shut her up and that pisses me off."

"The Knights know their mission. Leave them to their work."

I almost growled. "I knew it was them!" The Knights were a sect of anti-demon warriors, supposedly ratified by the Vatican. They worked to protect the world from demonic attack but their methods ... well, let's just say if a person suggested they should be subtler, they'd probably burn them at the stake whilst waving a bible in their face.

I clenched my fist. "She's an innocent in this. I'm going to help her."

"There are no innocents, Radshaw. Only shepherds and sheep."

"And what am I in that equation?"

"A sheep with ideas."

I sat back in the booth and hovered the beer near my mouth. "Are you going to help me, or do I have to drink this while it's your turn to speak?"

The baritone of his chuckle ravaged my

throat. **"You entertain me. For that reason, I will tell you where to go. I urge you, though - do not act on this. Allow the Knights to complete their mission."**

It was my turn to laugh through my mouth. "Dude, you really don't know me very well, do you?"

*****

"Boss, I'm serious. I don't think this is a good idea," said Amy in my ear. "This place doesn't even show up on Google maps. *Everything* shows up on Google maps."

I looked up at the dingy, monolithic tower block before me. It was like someone took the concept of humanity's absolute failure and rendered it in sixties-style architecture. Filth-framed holes, lined in jagged shards, outlined the gravestones of windows. Grey-brown dirt clad the building like a skin-fitting trench coat of grime and shit. I felt a shudder emanate from my head, shaking my bones from skull to tootsies. If anyone still lived in here, they'd have gone feral years ago.

"I don't recall," I said, breathing a visible sigh into the chill air, "saying I thought this was a good idea." The building rose proudly - if dirtily - from the surrounding rubble of its fellows like the last soldier of an outdated, utterly defeated army. If squalor and hate had a champion, I was about to climb its piss and syringe-riddled stairs.

A crackle in my ear told me signal reception was poor here. "Just be careful," said Amy before being cut off. My foot squelched on what looked like a blood-

streaked condom, shrivelled and sad like a dead rodent.
I kicked it away with an involuntary yelp.

"Fucking right," I muttered.

*Just keep climbing. You'll find what you need - or
it'll find you.* That's what The Bloke Down The Pub told
me. At the time, I assumed he was being melodramatic
but now I wasn't so sure. I walked into the cold embrace
of grey shadows, following the concrete hallway to the
bare stairs at the rear of the building. Overhead, a
fluorescent light flickered as it dangled from the ceiling -
a proper cliché, and entirely appropriate. Illuminating
nothing, it did at least serve to deafen me with its
caustic buzzing.

I hugged my long coat close and mounted the
first flight of stairs. They doubled back every half storey,
rising into blackness like giant, grimy pinking shears.
"You really are a prize Dickhead, Mike," I mumbled as I
went. "What kind of muppet willingly visits a place like
this?" I turned a corner and started a new flight, puffing
some big breaths. "Don't be such a pussy. Miss Guvern
needs your help. The Knights think killing her is the
solution, but you know she's just a symptom."

She'd come to me a few days ago, convinced
somebody was following her. I'd tried explaining my job
was usually to do the following myself but she was
adamant I could help. Money was rarer than intelligent
pop songs so I took the job. Since then, I'd been tailing
her everywhere. It was the easiest money I'd ever
made, until an oncoming truck took a suicidal plunge
onto the wrong side of the M1, turning her tiny car to
scrap. If the Knights thought that would put me off,
they were sorely mistaken. Now I was more determined

than ever to solve her case. It seemed clear these pitter-patters were a fundamental part of the problem, although I wondered why she'd not mentioned them when we first spoke. The Knights probably thought it meant she was possessed and needed a good killing-to, but I knew the hallmarks of being stalked when I encountered them.

"If you live here, I'm coming for you." I touched my hand against the shape of my gun in the large coat. "I'll make you leave her alone."

The building got darker as I ascended. My mobile phone's torch was as much use as a tissue airbag so I gave up after ten seconds of trying it and allowed my eyes to adjust to the gloom. I was on, perhaps, the tenth floor when I first heard something.

pitpat pitpat ... pitpat

I sniffed in a sharp breath and snapped my head to the side. The sound seemed to come from behind and to the side, off down the hall between flats, but there was no realistic source for it. I stood motionless for a few minutes, listening to the thunderous bass drum of my heart, until vague patterns of colour swirled before my eyes. Nothing - not beyond the vacant throb of my own consciousness. I let a seemingly endless breath leak out through my nose along with the tense set of my muscles - amazing, how long the human body can go without breathing when tension takes it. I lifted one foot and moved it towards the next step.

pitpat, pitpat.

From above! I rushed up the next few flights, using an arm to yank myself onward with the balustrade when my legs started turning to jelly. On the top floor, I paused to catch my breath, sending my gaze along the balcony hall to left and right then back again. There were no more stairs to climb so it was here or bust. A shadow flicked in the corner of my vision but I turned to see nothing. There was a fluttering sound like bat's wings but no sight to accompany it. With reluctance, my breathing and heartrate settled back to something approaching normal.

pitpat pitPAT! PIT!pat.

"For fuck's sake, just show yourself, will you?" I could hear the wobbly, high tone in my voice and hated it.

Silence. More fucking silence, choking and thick. For the first time, I understood how it could be deafening. With no aural or visual reference points, a lack of sounds was the same as the inability to hear - the end result was me having no clue what was happening around me. I strained my ears until phantom noises floated on my mental breeze but there didn't seem any point. Eventually, I gave up and moved along the balcony. A quick rub at the wall revealed the floor number - thirteen.

Of course it was.

'Wankers took me Mam,' proclaimed a hastily-scribbled line of graffiti. A little further on, I read, 'sick bitch in 1310.'

"I guess 1310's my destination."

I was passing some of those smashed windows as I traversed the balcony. Through them, the view looked correct but it was dull and muted, etched in browns like a landscape in a post-apocalyptic computer game. No sound floated in and no hint of motion disturbed the vista. I got the distinct feeling I wasn't in Kansas anymore. It occurred to me I hadn't checked the door at the front of this building. It'd been open so I wandered in. I hadn't checked for runes. Perhaps it was like that door I'd ventured through into the creepy old factory, leading somewhere grim and supernatural, scary and elsewhere. Leading somewhere *wrong*.

"PITPAT!"

"Stop doing that!" I damned near pissed myself as a spike of fear thrust down through my spine into my stomach. Before I realised I was toppling, the ground hit my knees.

It gets used to the pitter-patter. It opens its arms to the darkness. The voice shuddered through the air, reedy and sepulchral like a wet dalek. It sounded like a tape that got chewed once too often and it pierced my organs, soaking into me with rancid fervour. I coughed, holding onto my bladder and bowels to keep control of myself.

Still, I've always hated bullies.

"Pick on me all you want, arsehole. Just leave Miss Guvern alone. The lady's suffered enough."

Laughter rippled through me. It felt as if someone was beating my lungs like a dusty duvet. *It doesn't understand. It does not know whose door it knocks upon.*

I looked up to see a door before me - the last door on the balcony. 1310 was emblazoned on a bronze plaque above the letterbox, a greasy smudge beneath the number. Feeling numb, I reached up and rubbed it away with my thumb to reveal the writing beneath.

Guvern Family Residence.

Guvern feeds the pitter-patter. Guvern is our frieeeeeeend.

I heard a noise from inside the flat - a dull scrape like a chair sliding on stone flooring. Shadows moved and panic rippled through my chest. Something was inside, moving towards me, and I knew if I entered this place, I'd never leave. That didn't sit right with me. That didn't seem right at all.

So I ran like a cheerleader in a horror film.

*****

My footsteps echoed through the halls of St Thomas' hospital, muffled in my ears but drawing attention - I must have been walking more loudly than I realised. I'd been told my client was recovering and now resided in a close attention ward. When I strode into the room, a sensation all too familiar washed over me. All sound ceased and motion became subtle. Although there were other patients in the ward, she commanded all the attention. Even with one leg raised and white swathes cladding her bedridden form, she looked powerful and serious.

Probably due to the steely, unwavering glare she was levelling at me.

"What happened, Mr Radshaw?" she asked, her little-girl voice belying those ancient eyes. "Why didn't you protect me?"

I slumped into the chair next to her bed, matching her stare as I let my body flop - knees splayed and gut sticking out and *everything.* "You haven't been straight with me, Miss Guvern."

She batted her eyelashes coquettishly. "Whatever do you mean?"

"I think you knew it was the Knights following you. I think they'd finally caught up with you and you needed someone idiotic enough to try and keep them off you. I think you're less innocent than you make out."

She smiled. "And I think I want my money back."

"What's the pitter-patter?" I crossed my arms. Whoever or whatever she was, I wanted some answers.

"I was probably fourteen when the responsibility passed to me." She paused for a moment and her eyes wandered as though seeking a distraction before returning to me. She sighed. "It was a Sunday morning. I remember because it was cold as ice outside but bright and sunny. Why are Sunday mornings always sunny, Mr Radshaw?" When I just stared at her, she smiled and continued. "My mother called me into her bedroom. She was sweating and grey of skin, as though she'd been running until she collapsed."

I studied her face - determined but genuine, at once a little girl recalling a disturbing memory and a calculating woman deciding which secrets to keep.

"She told me she was barren. The pitter-patter of little feet in the hall normally woke her each morning. Today, it was the absence of it. Today, the pitter-patters were gone." Her eyes blinked and there were tears brimming. "It was my turn."

I tapped my foot, trying to ignore the twitching in my gut. "I'm not entirely certain I want to know, but I ask you again. What's the pitter-patter?"

"Miss Guvern really shouldn't have told you

about that. Sadly, she resisted unconsciousness a little longer than I." She looked deadly serious and I realised - at least as far as the speaker was concerned - she wasn't talking in the third person. "Some things are not for your ilk to know." A smile crawled from the creases of her face. "I've changed my mind, Mr Radshaw. You can keep your fee." A wince tugged briefly at her eyes. "You protected me for just long enough."

Something shifted under the covers of her hospital bed. Something jerky and alien. Something beneath her skin. My diaphragm heaved. I was very glad I hadn't eaten. The smile was now a broad grin on her face, a rictus of pain and triumph. I felt an enormous urge to punch her in it.

"Perhaps not," I said. "You see, I had a pretty good idea I was on the wrong side after visiting your family home." Her eyes widened as I got up and arranged my clothes before matching her stare. "So I made a phone call on the way here. Turns out, there are lots of people interested in your whereabouts."

Without waiting for a response, I strode towards the exit. At the ward entrance, a group of men in hospital porter's uniforms was waiting. With their bodybuilder figures and shaped facial hair, not to mention the suspicious shapes under their clothes, they weren't very convincing, but it'd got them far enough. As I passed, I exchanged a nod with one of them and they piled into the ward behind me. I heard the *sching* of unsheathing metal as I took my exit.

*****

The Kid n Fiddler seemed less intimidating this time round. As dingy and sticky as it was, a dark pub in deepest London couldn't hold a candle to a demonic tower block that whispered to its occupants. I paid my thirty silver for a rancid beer and headed straight for the shadowy corner. I knew I'd done the right thing, but I needed to know what I'd been dealing with. With luck, The Bloke Down The Pub would tell me.

I sucked on a cough sweet as I sat down, determined to give my throat as much armour as possible. Still, I couldn't protect myself from his word choice.

"You really are a fuckwit, Radshaw. If there were awards for not listening, you'd be holding the trophy. First class idiot."

"Hey thanks. I really needed a top-up for my self-loathing."

He chuckled and I coughed. **"Go home. Restore your sanity. The Knights finished their work in the hospital and you got out clean. There is nothing more to do."**

I sighed. "You know me better than that, Bloke. I have to know. Just tell me what the pitter-patter is."

"You know about the doors - the ancient portals between this world and the demon realms. They are but one route for them to enter. On this case, you encountered another. The Guvern family were conduits."

"I'm not certain I want you to, but please elaborate."

"The pitter-patter of tiny feet is the sound of massing demonspawn. Conduits are females in a

family line with the ability to channel demon children. Their role is one of distribution and release."

"So by 'channel' you mean..."

"Give birth, yes. Had you left Miss Guvern to her devices, St Thomas' would now be seething with misshapen devils and semi-formed beings. She used you, Radshaw. The Knights found her just days before her fruition and she used your sense of honour to keep them at bay."

I felt so weak, I almost drank a mouthful of my beer. "Are there more of these families - these conduits?"

The answer felt almost inevitable, growling from my throat with a sense of regret. **"Thousands."**

I stood up to leave. "Then I have a lot of work to do."

THE DEMON ASSASSIN

THE DEMON ASSASSIN

The bed was empty, but blood soaked the mattress, duvet, and pillows. The headboard sported a brain coat with a skull fragment polka-dot. Combined with the dripping curtains, squelching carpet and saturated armchair, the room looked like an abattoir for soft furnishings.

Just my luck - she'd been alive when we fell asleep.

I scratched my head, at a loss for how to react. Don't get me wrong, I wasn't calm. My heart was banging faster than a randy monkey, my veins felt like the ropes on a busy pulley system, and my bowels were setting up home in my shoes. No, I most certainly wasn't calm.

"You're in shock, Mike, my friend," I admonished myself. "What in the name of all that's fucked and blind are you going to do about this?"

Ring the police was what I should do, but they already thought I was nuts, and my preparatory mental narrator was pulling his hair out over how to phrase *that* phone call. *("Err, hi, yeah, I got laid last night for the first time in, no, not important ... Listen, there was this woman in my bed, now there's ... Look, some bad shit's gone down. Just when I get a moment of happiness- no, Mike, still not relevant ... SHE'S DEAD, MAN! There's blood everywhere and they took her skeleton!")*

Yep, definitely not calling the police.

I had to get out of my flat. A shower, taken with all the verve of a zombie on lithium, got most of the blood out of my hair but left the abiding odour of guilt. Could I have stopped this? I knew I was going to find out.

I checked, and my shoes were clean - more than I could say for the walls, the ceiling, and even my white paper light shade that my Mum got me for Christmas! I wouldn't be able to turn that on again without starting a new red light district.

I left my home - the grizzly (and indeed gristly) scene of the crime - in a hurry and sacrificed myself on the altar of London's fresh air.

*****

As I strolled, I munched on a sausage McMuffin. My conscience fainted but hey; a guy needs his breakfast.

"Come on, Mike," I muttered. "You're a detective. You can figure this out."

It's about time I introduced myself. Mike Radshaw's the name, and I've seen shit that'll turn you white. Sorry - I watched Ghostbusters last night with my now-dead date, and it's one of those films that leaves quotes floating in your head. I've faced down a randy demon with acid spunk, travelled to a sub-dimension to defeat a zombie army, and stopped a street gang from unleashing hell with bad language and kiddie porn. I've even averted a mass demon baby birthing. I make psychotherapists cry and I enjoy watching tennis.

I cut my professional teeth as a cop, and then did a stint following celebrities around. As protection, I mean - not as a stalker. Now I'm a dick, and sometimes that means private investigator. There's a guy I know only as Mr Black who seems wrapped up in all the weird shit I get caught up with. One day I'll find that bloke, and he won't enjoy it.

I pulled out my mobile phone, pressed the green button, and intoned, "Amy." The phone looked at me blankly. After two more attempts, I gave up and dialled her number, leaving big greasy finger prints all over the stupid touch screen.

"Radshaw's Investigations," answered my assistant, "your boggle is our bag. How may we help?"

I snorted a laugh into my phone. "Your boggle is our bag?"

"Oh, hi boss! I'm trying out new strap lines. You like?"

I sighed. "Even if you hadn't just made me blow scrambled egg out my nose, all over my shiny new phone, I don't think I'd be falling in love with that one."

"Okay," she said with a giggle. "I'll keep working on it. What's up, you not coming in today? Hangover, bruised coccyx, cat got piles again?"

"Listen, Amy. Something really nasty's happened. I think this is a black trouser case." 'Black trouser' was the code we had for the really fucked up situations; the ones where I thought Mr Black might be involved, along with very scary situations that may dictate underwear replacements. "I need a meeting with the Knights."

I heard the clatter of a keyboard under duress, then Amy's voice, all hint of levity gone. "Okay, boss. I'll set it up and text you a location."

"Thanks, Amy." There was a brief silence.

"Mike?"

"Yeah?"

"You need to talk?"

I paused in a shop doorway, biting my lip. "She was a nice person, Amy. She didn't deserve this."

"Understood. I'll get you that meeting, and be careful. Good bosses are hard to replace."

*****

Every city has secret nooks and crannies, quiet pockets of peaceful solitude tucked away from the bustle behind buildings, beneath roads, and down unassuming alleys. They might be quads with fountains, secluded gardens, or forgotten yards of defunct factories. London has graveyards. If you're not standing in one, chances are you're strolling over another. The foundations of London are packed tight with bones and victims, departed souls and crushed dreams.

I gazed across the small field of worn stone nubs before me, their stilted forms thrust tragically from the earth like trees that didn't make it. What a venue for a meeting! A tiny church lurked to one side, nestled in the shadows of buildings hundreds of years its junior.

The chilly breeze pushed my hands into my long-coat pockets then carried a cough to my ears. I turned to see a shadowy figure in a trench coat identical to mine with the collar turned up, a cliched fedora perched atop its head.

"A chill day," intoned the gap between hat and collar.

I couldn't resist answering, "Grey Squirrel, is that you?"

The figure sank visibly. "Very funny, Mr Radshaw. I'm here at great personal risk. What business have you with the Knights?"

"If you set off bombs in London, even the really crummy parts, a certain notoriety comes with the turf. You have to expect the authorities to hunt you when you come off like a terrorist."

The shadow sighed and, when he spoke again, the voice was noticeably less deep. "Look, Radshaw, I only have a few minutes. Please get to the point."

"I met a nice lady last night. She was kind to me when she didn't have to be. Now she's a pool of blood and assorted fragments, with a missing skeleton. I want to know what did it," my hands shook, nails digging deep into palms, and I knew my face had gone deathly pale, "and I want to know where it lives."

The Knight inhaled sharply as I spoke but remained silent. I'd first encountered the order when I nearly died destroying a building with a huge bomb to close a dimensional gateway. I trapped a host of demons behind the door that day. It turned out the bomb was set by the Knights, and they knew more about the forces I'd faced than anybody else, even if their methods were to subtlety what German porn is to a love letter.

"You know something," I said. "What?"

"I'm so sorry, Radshaw. We had no idea it was here for you."

"WHAT? What is here for me?" My words fired towards the knight like bursts of angry smoke in the cold air.

He sat down on a tribute to a long-dead Londoner. "Something big is in town. A powerful entity, from one of the really deep planes. We suspect an assassin."

I sat down opposite. An assassin? What the hell did a demon assassin look like? More to the point, if I was being honest, did I really want to find out? "But why tangle dicks with me?" I asked.

A snort fired a white puff from the shadowy figure. "You've been putting out adverts in all the papers, asking for soldiers to face 'the dark'. Did you think that wouldn't get noticed?"

"It got noticed, alright - by every nutjob from Wimbledon to Upton Park! I've been buried in lunatics ever since I had that ridiculous idea."

"Irrelevant," said the knight with a shrug. "The point is, you drew attention that is definitely not wanted; you're a bigger threat than our order has managed to be in centuries."

I pretended to weigh my thoughts but I knew what I was going to do. When Lucifer fucks with your girlfriend, there's only one appropriate response.

I looked the knight in the eyes, or at least where I reckoned them to be. "Where do I find this thing, and how do I kill it?"

"Before I answer that, Radshaw, how are your fingers - the ones that got flayed when you put your hand through a portal?"

"They look fine to the eye - not even a scar - but I wake up every morning and they sting like I've spent all night fingering Satan's arsehole, and let me tell you; the bastard guffs acid."

The knight's shoulders shook, but they did so silently. "How eloquent," he replied eventually, "but that pain means something potentially positive. You have a connection to the other side, Radshaw. Their rancid taint has infested your hand."

I gave him my best 'sickened' expression. "Apart from meaning I'll now eat one-handed for the rest of my life, how exactly does that help me?"

"Simple, my mad friend; it means you can open their doors."

*****

'*We will shortly be arriving at ...* **London Charing Cross** *... where this service will terminate,"* announced the train speakers.

"Terminate what?" I muttered, trying to ignore my shaking hands. I'd have loved to blame them on the train vibrations but I wasn't in that much denial.

"Please ensure you take all your personal belongings with you when leaving the train, and leave nothing in the train, or on the station."

I watched the London Eye turning ponderously through the skyline as we crossed the Thames. "Shouldn't that be 'ON the train, or IN the station'?"

A fellow passenger tittered and I realised I'd been speaking aloud. If I wasn't careful, the men in white coats would soon be after me. If the Knights' information was reliable, there was a 'currently active' door secluded beneath the platforms of Charing Cross train station, and it was most likely a portal to the lair of the demon assassin. Getting to the station was the easy part - the greater challenge was descending beneath it without being noticed.

When the doors opened and dull-eyed commuters poured onto the platform, I hung back and slunk to the rear of the train. Before I had time to think better of it, I stepped off the platform edge, dropped to my front, and squeezed into the space between train wheels and platform foundations. As I army-crawled towards the front end of the train, my shoulders and backside scraping filthy concrete and filthier train, the scars on my fingers throbbed with ever-increasing fury.

"Looks like the knight was right," I whispered.

Footsteps filled the air above me as passengers boarded the stationary train, now preparing for its new destination. I quickened my crawl as best I could in the narrow space, not liking my chances if the train started to move while I was still there. There was supposed to be an opening beneath the platform, near to the ticket barriers at the front of the train. That meant I had two more carriage-lengths to crawl before I reached it. There was a deep electronic whirr filling my world and raising the hairs on my arms as I approached the front carriage. An announcer was listing the service's destinations and the doors were bleeping to warn of their imminent closure. Sod it! I bashed along, tearing up my elbows and knees, and as soon as I felt air open up beneath the platform I threw myself head-first into the opening. Behind my heels, train wheels screeched into motion.

Breath echoing all around me, wounds throbbing,

I felt myself slipping down a steep incline in a world of total black. Before I even caught enough breath to scream, I lost all contact with ground and simply fell. Air brushed at the backs of my ears, and moments later my ribs crashed against my lungs as I slammed into the ground. Pain exploded through my body, and then there was nothing.

*****

I awoke and the world was a sickly yellow-green. If disease teamed up with asphyxiation to create a colour, this would be the creepy, gloomy result. If my bleary vision was to be believed, I was at the bottom of a rough, dirt-lined chute, and looming over my aching form was a repulsively familiar door. I'd seen its like before; dirty, ancient timber in a deep brown, pitted and cracked but more solid than steel. Scrawled across it like a mass spider graveyard were runes, written by the hand of unkempt chaos. What I hadn't witnessed before was the glow, emanating from those scribblings, pulsing with ponderous irregularity as though fed by a sick heartbeat.

My throbbing fingers were roaring at me with furious agony, drowning out even my torn elbows and bruised back. I shoved myself upright and faced down the hideous door with a defiant sniff. Shaking hand held before me, I winced and pushed my way through.

Previously, passing through such portals had felt like shoving my whole body through a vat of dough. This time, my hand pressed against the solid door, and then proceeded to swing it open. As yellowy-green light filled my vision, a waft of air pregnant with rot and decay assailed my nostrils. My heart rate accelerated into mad overdrive, but I stepped forward nonetheless. At this stage, there was no going back.

After just two steps, I was in an open space. A rock ceiling soared above me, light emanated from flaming torches set into the ground, sand covered the floor, and I was sure I could hear crashing ocean in the distance. The cave smelled like a cask-conditioned curry fart and every lungful of it made me want to retch. Yellow water dripped from glistening stalactites to collect in bubbling pools upon the ground. I could see for perhaps a hundred feet, and then the whole cave turned a corner and disappeared into darkness.

I checked my gun in its shoulder holster - no use against the assassin, the knight had said. No use, that was, unless I was able to weaken it first.

"You're good, Mike," I muttered through shuddering breaths. "You can take this. Just think about that poor woman." Anger flooded me and I strode forward on a wave of righteous vim.

As I turned the corner, I found myself in a round rock chamber. Ahead, the cave narrowed into a tunnel. Dark sounds of breath and splutter drifted on the air from the dark opening. When I looked to one side, my heart almost fell into my shoes.

There she was - the kind lady. The first person who'd given me happiness in so long that I'd been amazed the plumbing all functioned. She'd been no contender for the Next Summer Catalogue, but when you're doing rather than browsing, it's amazing how little that matters. Now she was no contender for anything - a glistening skeleton hanging on the wall. Some of her organs were still caught up in the bone scaffold and ragged strips of tissue clung like matted crimson fur to her frame. Her permanent grin mocked me from above.

"Motherfucker," I sighed, tears dripping down my cheeks and splashing onto my balled fists. "You dirty motherfucker!"

A laugh suffused the air, thick with sticky saliva. I say 'laugh', but it sounded more like a giant Darth Vader belching. I'd woken up the demon assassin, and he sounded mightily pissed.

The knight's passing advice rang in my ears. *"He took her skeleton to lure you, to bring you into his domain, but the very thing he relies on - the sense of love and loyalty you feel for her - is his weakness. Show him, express your love before him, and he will not be able to face you. Show him not your anger, Radshaw, for that is what he sups upon. Show him instead your sensitive side."*

I turned my back on the doorway he was approaching through. I got the distinct feeling that a powerful demon assassin was not going to be a pretty sight, and the inevitable terror I'd feel if I saw him was not the emotion I wanted to project. Instead, I approached the skeleton on the wall. Reaching up, I lifted her from the nails that held her in place and cradled her tacky remains in my arms. One eye socket still had the remnants of an eyeball in it, so I focused on the torn cornea. Behind me, the breathing noise went from muffled to fresh and I thought I felt a draught teasing my clothes.

"I don't know what love is, really," I said to the ragged skull. "I've seen it, heard about it, watched it on TV, but I've never really understood it. Perhaps you were the one, or perhaps we were just destined for one blissful night." Another chuckle came from behind, and this time my hair danced to its tune. The demon's breath stank like a mass grave in a heat wave, but something hard inside my gut stopped me from gagging.

"All I know is I was very fond of you, and you didn't deserve to be ripped apart by some dirty demon with a grudge. Sleep soundly, fair lady."

With that, I leaned forward and kissed her. There was half an upper lip stuck to some gristle, so that pressed into my mouth, and other than that it was teeth and bone all the way. *This is either the most romantic moment imaginable or the worst 'bush tucker trial' in the history of existence!* Despite my repulsion, a sensation of deep peace filtered through me.

Behind me, a demon roared in anguish. I could almost feel the waves of my emotions, pounding against the assassin's hate like tidal waves on a coastal wall. I laid the skeleton gently upon the cave floor, allowing my tears to dapple the blood-cakes skull. She was innocent – more innocent than I'd ever be. Gall rose in my throat and a fresh howl crashed against my back.

I drew my gun from its holster, imagining the peaceful life I might have had.

Then I turned and emptied every bullet into a head the size of my chest that seemed to be formed entirely of teeth. I think I screamed. I think I cursed. I think I poured my soul into killing that vile creature that so casually rent my life. My vision blurred as my finger moved, darkness swamping me as anger burst through my system, finally allowed release.

Whatever I did, it worked, because when I came to my senses I was ankle-deep in the dark sludge I knew was their blood. My head was full of scrambled insanity but, somewhere beneath it all, I knew I'd won.

I couldn't go back the way I'd come - there was no way for me to climb that chute back to Charing Cross station. Instead, I headed deeper into the huge demon's lair. Tunnels gave way to more tunnels until everything became a blur of dirt and gloom. All I knew was I could still hear the ocean, and it seemed to be getting louder. That thought sustained me, and I pushed on until I couldn't feel my feet and every breath I drew felt like nails dragged across the back of my throat.

When I crashed into another door covered with glowing runes, it took me a moment to realise what had happened. Raising my tainted hand, I pushed it open feebly and fell through into fresh air.

I know I staggered more, but not where or for how long. I walked until I simply toppled over onto my face. It was only when my mouth filled with saltwater I realised I was on a beach - a pebble beach, my bruises informed me. I could hear feet slapping in shallow water and then hands grabbing me and turning me over. I coughed a spray of brine across my face.

"Is this Hell?" I croaked as light speared into my eyes, refusing to allow me vision.

"Nah, mate," came the reply. "This is Brighton!"

I laughed until the coughing drowned my voice. "I learned something," I shouted. "I found a new way to fight them."

"Fight who?" asked the saviour voice.

"Trust me," I said, feeling my resolve hardening like quick-dry cement. "You don't want to know."

MICHAEL E BELL

MIKE RADSHAW AND THE BLACK DAWN

A novella

CHAPTER 1 – THE DEMON OF DEATH

The cards had been dealt. I found myself looking Death in his hideous face, inked meticulously by someone with a morbid imagination and way too much time on their hands.

"I predict," I said, my words lost quickly to the plethora of velvet drapery and tense atmosphere, "the artist behind these cards wears black lipstick."

The deafening silence I got in response told me I faced a tough audience. I slapped my hands down on the small table, causing candlelight to flicker and cards to shift. Death still stared implacably, oblivious to his disrespectful treatment.

"He paints his nails black," I continued. "He finds corpses romantic, believes in the beauty of depression, and thinks Marilyn Manson is a lightweight, over commercialised pussy." My words sank into the atmosphere of the tent interior. If I hadn't travelled there, I would never have believed I was currently sitting on the edge of Clapham Common, in a circus stall.

"Mock not the grim reaper, Mister Radshaw," said the old gypsy woman sitting opposite. If a voice could be labelled 'sepulchral', hers was living proof. She made Vin Diesel sound like a chipmunk castrato. On helium. "He sees your soul and he craves its flavour."

"What, eight pints of Bombardier and a Doner kebab with a doner list three pages long?"

She stabbed me with the kind of glare that makes serial killers cry and milk curdle in the udder.

"Your droll tongue flaps like a dirty rag in the

breeze, but you do not hide your fear from me. The terror sweats from your pores, infesting you with its stench."

"That'll be the hangover." I tried to match her stare, squinting across the dimly lit space. It was no use, and she was dead right. I felt like a spotty teenager telling Mr T I'd just got his daughter pregnant. In his bed. And I wiped my junk on his curtains. I sighed inwardly.

Mike Radshaw's the name, and you've suffered the misfortune of stumbling on my life in progress - sorry about that. In my time as a cop and a PI, I've come to know demons both literal and figurative. I'm just stupid enough to poke my nose where it's not wanted, and so far it hasn't been clawed off. I've opened doors to places so FUBAR they make Tower Hamlets look like Utopia, and lived to tell the tales. I've faced demon assassins and zombie babies, even taken on a kiddie-fiddling street gang.

None of that helps when you're staring Death in his disturbingly well-drawn face.

"You came to me, Mister Radshaw," croaked the crone. "Forces gather in the shadows and you seek a torch, but only black ink can obscure what is written."

I sat back in the chair and let my arms dangle. "Is that supposed to help me?"

She smiled with all the warmth of a glacier wearing sunglasses. "You have Death's attention. He is drawn to the cadence of your flame. In the lonely night, a star will shine forever."

"That will not do," I whispered.

"Hah!" she exclaimed. I actually jumped and,

feeling foolish, sat forward again. Shadows slithered through the grooves in her face but nothing could distract from the eyes. They beamed; green and bloodshot by booze, but wild with belief. She extended a hand. "Cross my palm."

I hesitated, but knew I had no choice. I dropped a small plastic bag into her clutch. Hair from each zone of my body, sputum, blood and semen. And no, I didn't ask why.

"Seek the light's wake, Mister Radshaw," she said. "All manner of thing may follow a star, but who will look behind it?"

*****

The tiny fingers gripped my thumb, pulling with insistent fervour. I resisted and the baby chugged out one of those delighted giggles that make the whole world smile. It filled my little office with sorely-needed levity.

"He's sooo cute!" said Amy. Assistant, confidant and frequent life-saver, Amy ran my PI business while I did the easy part. She was like a sat nav for my entire life, ushering me from one place to the next with assurance and aplomb. She had a better voice than the average in-car system, though, and more soul than I'd encountered in anybody else I'd ever met.

"What the fuck am I supposed to do with a baby?" I muttered. Gazing along the length of my outstretched arm into huge, blue eyes in a round face, all I felt was helpless. I'd like to say I couldn't imagine anyone wanting to hurt this fragile, young life, but I've seen too much to believe that.

Amy cooed down at the child, extracting an unfettered grin.

"The Knights gave him to you for a reason," she said. "The guy that dropped him off looked terrified. They can't protect him, Mike, and they think you can. That's a compliment, in my book."

I snorted. "If that's a compliment, politicians are always honest and spin doctors are just high-end deejays." The tiny fist tugged again at my thumb. "Who are you, little man?" I asked. "How did you end up with the Knights, and what evil thing wants you dead?"

I got a wet smile in response. The Knights were a secret order who claimed to be affiliated with the Vatican. I'd first encountered them after detonating a bomb in a disused factory to seal a demon portal. As it turned out, it was their bomb and I'd finished the job for them. They'd been fighting forces for centuries that I was only just coming to understand, but their methods were stuck in the dark ages. Why plug a hole with a cork when you can collapse a building on top of it? These days, we had an uneasy truce. We shared information and, it now seemed, babies.

I wondered if the ever-elusive 'Mister Black' was involved at all. He seemed behind or linked to all the crap I had to deal with. Originally, he'd been just another client, but now I was certain he was the enemy. Mister Black; not that original as bad guy labels went, but evil comes with a limited colour palette.

"What did the tarot reader say?" asked Amy.

"She said I'm as fucked as a cute prisoner with a habit of dropping soap."

She sighed. "If this baby's first word is some hideous expletive, you'll be to blame, boss-o-mine."

"The gypsy told me I'm too clear a target," I said quietly. "As things stand, I'm like a crosshair, pinpointing this kid's location to every dark force in play." I looked Amy straight in the eyes, and I could see she knew what this meant as well as I did.

"I need to go dark."

"I'll set it up," she said in a tiny voice.

I put my best sardonic smile in place. "Tell me I'm not insane, Amy."

"I'm not insane, Amy." Her face betrayed no hint of a smile.

"Thanks."

*****

"Man, you got narrow shoulders," said Raffer, pulling on my recently doffed trench coat.

"Just be grateful I'm not making you wear my undies," I replied. "Now, you know what needs to happen?"

"Yeah, yeah," replied the actor as he sniffed at my coat shoulder and grimaced dramatically. "I's you, at least until the money's run out. Man, you ever washed this thing?"

"No, and it's important you don't, either. It's not enough, you looking like me, Raf. You need to act the part down to my toes. That means the smelly coat, three-day stubble, and a sarcasm level higher than Simon Cowell's waistband. This investigator needs to believe you're me, so you'll be working out of my office with Amy, and she'll get you on a real-looking case."

Raffer was an old acquaintance, a decent actor who never got a big break and bore an uncanny resemblance to yours truly. That made him ideal when I needed someone to represent me at boring-looking meetings or as a decoy if I thought I was being followed. We were at his apartment in Brixton - an address I was reasonably sure would not be under any sort of surveillance.

He grinned at me. "So, what if I's better at Peeing in the I than you?"

"I'll retire a happy man."

"This dude you got following you - he dangerous?"

I kept my face straight as a wave of guilt washed over me like an unwelcome flush. "He's just a rival, hired by a disgruntled ex-client. I can't risk him finding out the case I'm working on. You're cool, man."

"Aight, no problems, Radshaw." He started ushering me to the door.

"Don't forget the baby - I left the pushchair downstairs."

He gave me a look like I'd just farted in his coffee. "Man, I thought you was joking about the baby."

"If I was joking, I'd have said two condoms are walking past a gay bar. One goes to the other, 'let's go in and get shit-faced.'"

Raffer grabbed up the 'baby'; a realistically weighted, moving doll that - frankly - freaked me out, but it had to be believable. "You a homophobe, man," he muttered resentfully.

"Nah," I said as I opened his door, "I just like shit jokes."

*****

"You were not entirely honest with me, Mister Radshaw."

If I had a list of things I didn't want to hear my phone say to me, that would definitely have been on it, but it seemed the fortune-telling crone had left me a voicemail message. That I was listening to it for a second time probably made me a masochist.

"You did not tell me you were with child." I grimaced at her choice of words, and hoped she'd just picked a strange way to phrase it. I mean, the belly's got some roundness - no denying it - but I put that down to the aforementioned ale. "You must visit me again, detective. There is much you should know. This you get for free: Death is a demon. That is, the Death you see anthropomorphised in a cloak, clutching a scythe. You saw his likeness on my card, staring into your soul. Of course, he is much uglier in person. You need help. Forces are in play that you can neither conceive nor combat. The Prophecy has been invoked. For the rest, you must cross my palm again. I will be expecting you. END OF MESSAGE. TO-"

I terminated the call with my forehead and slipped my phone into a pocket.

I shook my other hand into a plastic bag then sealed it up. One more payment for the gypsy, one last chance to find out what was going on before I started putting adverts in the paper. I believed I had to keep this child safe, but curiosity was burning my gut like a Vindaloo with extra onions. For a week now, Raffer had been masquerading as me, pushing and carrying his fake baby around London and being very obvious about making 'routine enquiries'. No person or thing had taken the bait.

In the meantime, I'd spoken to every scrote, contact, informant and random stranger I could get my hands on. Nobody knew or was admitting the truth. The Knights had gone underground - probably literally - and the better informed shopkeepers from Soho's shadier alleys were conveniently on holiday.

I flushed the loo I'd been perched on and secreted the bag in an inside pocket. Emerging from the cubicle, I took the risk of washing my hands in the toilets at Victoria train station. There were many things I'd rather have touched than the tap, such as a leprous tramp with halitosis and a psychotic temper, or a used condom from a council estate tower block's stair well, but needs must when you've just been cramming various bodily excreta into a sandwich bag.

I shouldered the backpack with the baby, wincing at the weight. I was certain the pack itself weighed far more than the good-natured, thankfully sleepy child ensconced within. He'd been so good I almost didn't mind his company any more. I'd come to quite enjoy the feeding, burping, and cheer-up rituals.

"You can keep the nappy-changing, though," I muttered to myself. "There are some things nobody should have to encounter close up."

As I rode a night train to Clapham and the stars

presided over another barmy London summer, I tried to think of any alternative options. I really didn't want to expose this baby to the gypsy woman and her creepy cards, but she was the only one who seemed to have any clue what was occurring. I'd have far more chance of protecting the baby if I knew what from, and why I needed to.

I was approaching Clapham Common when the sight before me left me stumbling to a halt.

"Fuck my arse!"

Flickering lights splashed across the scene like strobe effects in a James Cameron flick. The gypsy woman's tent was gone, replaced by a vision that would make Quentin Tarantino shiver. Clearly, film directors would do well to stay clear of my head right now.

Great streamers of blood burst across the grass in a spray pattern thirty feet wide, their surfaces reflecting black and red alternately as the blue emergency lights atop cop cars and ambulances illuminated them. In the centre of the carnage was the small table I'd rested my hands on a week ago, now adorned with a pile of internal organs that weren't internal any more. Snakes of intestine spilled between surface and ground. In a sign that I found all too familiar, the skeleton was missing. From the distance, I could see a small rectangle perched atop the grisly heap. I didn't need to get any closer to know what it was; the death card, placed as a message.

My stomach tried to bundle my shoes and I was heartily glad I'd not eaten recently. What in fuck's name was I up against?

It was then, as I stood dumbly, that my phone

rang with that default Nokia tune that can turn half the population of a train carriage into psychopaths on the spot - exactly why I hadn't changed it. I fumbled it from my pocked and slid my finger across its screen to answer.

"Mike!" Amy's voice, thin and breathless. She was either terrified, exhausted, or in great pain. I was back in the game instantly.

"What's happened? Tell me you're alright!"

"He came here, Mike, Talking about 'The Prophecy' and sacrifices that must be made. He came for the baby."

My cheek felt cold and wet against the phone's surface. "Fuck that for the moment, Amy. Are you okay?"

"I'm fine, Mike, just got the shakes. Listen, I told him everything. He knows Raffer's location, and he's heading there now. It's an ancient church just off Horseferry Road, SW1. I'm sorry, Mike. I didn't know what else to do; I had to warn you."

The relief rushing through my system felt like dipping my toes in a cold stream during a heat-wave. "What did he look like?"

"A guy in a black suit, perfect hair, bright red eyes. He scared the shit out of me, Mike. He never threatened, just asked questions in a calm voice that made me wet my knickers. I don't know what he is, but you'd better know what you're doing if you plan to face him."

"You did the right thing, Amy. I couldn't live with myself if you got hurt. I know that church - I'll head there now. I just arrived at the gypsy's tent, and someone's made mincemeat out of her. Literally. If you don't hear from me by six, call every fucking cop in the Met and send them to that church!"

*****

As I sneaked up to the church door, I felt like the last fart in a half hour crapping session - behind in every way imaginable. I hated playing catch-up on a case, especially when my neck was on the line. It was now four in the morning, and the dull grey sky was casting a pall across London as pre-dawn took hold.

There's a magic to that half-light that makes sights seem shrink-wrapped and sounds incorporeal. The baby slept in his backpack, a situation for which I was extremely grateful. I'd considered leaving him somewhere safe, until I realised there wasn't anywhere safe. To get to the baby, they'd have to get through me. That would have to suffice.

I looked closely at the door and knew there were dark runes ingrained in the wood. They were hiding, but I could feel it. There was an almost intolerable mental pressure emanating from the ancient portal. Nobody would be able to open this door.

Unluckily for me, I'm not nobody. I placed my scarred hand upon the door's surface - the hand which had been flayed to the bone by a demon's claws. There was no resistance, and I pushed it open as quietly as I could manage, slipping it shut behind me.

As I slunk through the darkness, sticking to the deepest shadows at the edges of the nave, I heard voices. There, standing behind the lectern atop a dais, was my doppelganger Raffer, a man whose only crime was looking like me. He was looking down at a figure wearing a black suit, standing between the front rows of pews, his back to me.

"Relinquish the Angel's get!" said the suit in a tone like thunder's older brother.

Raffer looked down with an exaggerated bemused expression. "Assuming you made sense, mate, which you don't, I'm about as likely to do what you say as a seagull is to fly backwards."

I rolled my eyes - Raffer wouldn't fool anyone with such lame comebacks!

"I am not here to tolerate your sarcasm, Radshaw. Give me the baby."

My jaw dropped open in affront, but I managed to stay quiet. This was the whole reason for hiring Raffer - so I could hide behind his facade.

"I'm not giving you anything," said the actor, but his voice sounded shaky. I couldn't blame the poor guy.

"And yet you will," whispered the suit, his voice carrying despite its quietness. "I will take him, and snuff his infant spark from existence. He cannot be allowed to live. So says The Prophecy."

Raffer looked lost and I ached to join in, to confront this terrible monster in a man's guise. Instead, I stepped further back into darkness until I was touching the door, ready to bolt. I swear I felt a little part of me die inside right then.

"No," managed the actor in a tiny voice.

"YES!" The suit bulged suddenly and billowed into a cloak shape as the figure wearing it grew to more than eight feet in height. Tendrils of ragged cloth flapped away from his form like fabric tongues, licking hungrily at the church floor. From somewhere, he was holding a scythe with shining blade and gnarled, knotted haft. Whatever his face now looked like, it did a serious number on Raffer, who collapsed to his knees and blubbed for mercy.

Of course, he is much uglier in person.

Something clicked inside, a connection I should have made a long time ago, and a whisper escaped my lips.

"Mister Black, I presume."

The figure strode forward and the scythe swung down with implacable force, severing Raffer in a diagonal cut from left shoulder to right hip. His body flopped in two, pissing buckets of blood and bursting organs across the floor. The Death demon knelt down and I saw a hand formed entirely from foot-long thorns grip the actors' head.

"What? You are not Radshaw! This cannot be - the Prophecy!"

On a whim, I wanted to grab the bag of excreta from my pocket and splat its various contents on the floor. *'See that, staining your floor? You can kiss it. That's the fuck I don't give about your prophecy!'* But I knew I couldn't - there was too much at risk. Instead I slunk through the shadows and quietly made my escape.

As I descended the church steps into a burgeoning dawn, a terrifying voice thundered.

"I'll come for you, Radshaw. I'll find you!"

I'd successfully protected the sleeping child on

my back, the young creature that might be an angel. But at what cost, and for how long? There was one thing I knew beyond doubt, and it mapped me on a course of utter terror and abject uncertainty:

This was not over.

CHAPTER 2 – THE DARK KNIGHTS

As dusk descended over London like a lead storm cloud, I stirred my coffee and squinted at the sun's progress. Between the thoroughly eviscerated fortune teller who helped my cause and the bisected actor who'd posed as me, I was rapidly running out of allies. As night stole its way across the landscape, a sense of black dread invaded my thoughts.

I'd spent the day trying to get hold of anyone who might help me, but to no avail. The baby I'd been given to protect had spent most of the time sleeping, even when I started examining him for signs of wings. The Death demon, or grim reaper, or Mr Black - he scared the crap out of me regardless of what I chose to call him - had called it 'angel's get'. Did angels have babies? I frowned, unsure if I even believed in angels, but when you've seen zombies, demons, and sub-dimensions, a divine creature with a striking resemblance to Ben Affleck just seems like par for the course.

I shuffled closer to the window and pressed my forehead to the glass, enjoying its coolness. My office was crummier than a bread graveyard and so typical you couldn't walk from one side to the other without tripping over the cliches. That meant dreary, wood-panel decor, piles of paper so tall they got used as stools, and a light that flickered at ominous moments. It did, however, give me a view over the city, even if it was through a greasy dirt filter.

"If the world spent the rest of eternity in darkness, would we cope?" My voice sounded dull to my ears, even with the bassy reverberation from the window. "If our shadows stood in front of us instead of behind, if the sun became a black void in the sky and the air was packed with death and malice, and all the shit we saw in our nightmares became dreams of relief ... Would we survive?"

Amy tutted behind me. "You can be a morbid bastard sometimes, boss. Snap out of it!"

"I feel like an arsehole, Amy. I've handled this case with all the sensitivity of a concrete dildo. It's no wonder I feel sore. Raffer's decorating the floor of a church in Horseferry Road, and the fortune teller's deader than Bernard Manning's underpants. I've never seen anything like this Death demon - not even that fuck-faced assassin compared. I can't keep you safe, Amy, and I can't protect this baby."

"Do you really think it's Mr Black?" Her voice seemed uncharacteristically meek and I glanced towards her. She shook - subtly, but I was looking close. I didn't know if she'd told me everything about her encounter with Death, but I knew I'd give my right arm to keep her from going through it again.

"I'm certain of it."

We were matching stares in mutual acknowledgement of fear when the phone rang and I almost pissed myself in shock.

I was closer, so I grabbed the receiver and said, "Radshaw's Investigations - we pee ourselves so you don't have to."

"You're fired, Radshaw. We want the baby back."

"What, no small talk? Who the fuck is this?"

There was a sigh at the other end. "This is Sir Banbury, of the Knights. We have changed our minds about your task, Mr Radshaw. Please return the child to us immediately. You will be paid for your time until now."

His voice had the strain of somebody under duress, though he was trying to sound commanding to cover it. A thousand thoughts belted through my head at once. Not only were the Knights back on the scene, they were contacting me. Whilst it was possible they simply believed I was no longer up to the task, my gut was playing death metal riffs on my heart strings. When my instincts interfere with my biology, I make a point of listening. Somebody had got to the Knights, and I thought I knew who.

"Enough with the theatrics," I said. "I'm sure that voice usually has people flapping like a foreskin at a brit milah, but I don't frighten so easily. You want to see me, I want to see you, so tell me where to go."

There was a heavy breath over the phone followed by a muffled discussion. Then Sir Banbury's voice said, "The Buerk and Dragon, as soon as you can."

With a click, the line went dead.

I grabbed my coat from the old fashioned hanger by the door and threw a look at Amy. "No way I'm giving this baby back to the Knights. Something's spooked them. Without any other leads, I'm going to find out what or who it is. Keep him safe, Amy, and if you so much as have a weird or scary thought, get the fuck out of here. Go to my mum's place - she knows who you are - and text me something meaningless that won't give away your destination."

She nodded, her expression nervy but resolute. "Watch it, boss. I don't trust them."

*****

As I entered the Knights' safe house, I felt about as welcome as diarrhoea on the space shuttle. Silent faces stared from the shadows of hoods in the pools of darkness at the edges of the common room. The Buerk and Dragon was an ancient pub down a dismal alley in one of those areas of London that feels like the dark ages never ended. Hiding in a back street that sane people didn't know about, it should have died of financial starvation years ago.

There was fear in every gaze I met - the kind of primal terror that makes Wes Craven's best work look like Disney. Mr Black had put the willies up these guys something rotten, and that made me nervous. If fear makes a man do strange things, the Knights were about as rational as psychos in hockey masks at summer camp. And they ran a machete shop.

"Where is the angel child?" growled a voice from behind the bar. I looked into bright blue eyes beneath a blond crew cut. I gulped, recognising the offspring of a zealot and a crunchy nut cornflake when I saw one.

"And you are?" I noted with relief that my voice was steady and loaded with sarcasm; just how I like it.

His blond eyebrows drew together in a scowl. "I am Sir Wilberford, the new Deacon around here, and I asked you a question." Wilberford had a jaw like a monster truck bumper and an expression like Ray Winstone with his bollocks crushed in a vice. Against all sense, I decided to turn the handle.

"He's somewhere safe, as opposed to here. I take

my charges seriously, Wilberford. You're not getting a sniff of the baby until I'm satisfied of your motives."

I'd have said it wasn't possible, but his eyes widened and his voice roared louder. "The Angrath is not your concern, Radshaw! It must be handed to the Black One, there is no other option."

I walked over to the bar to show I wasn't intimidated. It wasn't true, but I was damned if I'd let him see that. I also got a moment to think. The Knights I knew were loopier than a slinky on a rollercoaster, but giving a baby to a demon just wasn't in their nature. Something had occurred here beyond a change of heart. And what the fuck was an Angrath? I placed my hands on a sticky bar mat and matched stares with the Arian Sir Wilberford, fighting the urge to tell him Father Adolf was proud.

"You're having a giraffe, aren't you? I always knew you guys were a couple of tits short of a whorehouse, but this is taking the piss." I looked round the dingy pub for effect. "The guy who dropped the baby off at my office thought there were other options. Where is he?"

"Sir Gentry has ... retired."

I scrunched the bar mat in a fist as a sickening hunch did the same to my gut. "Permanently?"

"Medically." Wilberford didn't bat an eyelid as he spoke, giving nothing away.

"And what, exactly, will Mr Black do with this 'Angrath' if he gets it?"

The Knight's face remained utterly impassive. "What must be done to avert the Black Dawn we will face if we anger him. Radshaw, even you must know there are forces we should not meddle with; the primal drivers that shape existence. It is Black's day, his time of dominance, and that means we must capitulate. It is in his power and his remit to turn off the sun. If we defy him, he will render this plane a barren darkness ruled over by the eldritch bones of humanity."

The anger had been building in me as I listened to Wilberford's tirade. "Nice speech, mate, but I don't buy it. If he could do that, he would have. And any force that demands the sacrifice of tots, whatever you might call them, damned well deserves to be meddled with."

Wilberford sighed. "Debate is irrelevant, Radshaw. He will have the baby. Indeed," he turned to cast a significant look at the clock on the wall behind the bar. "Yes, I'd say he probably already does."

In a heartbeat, my lungs turned to ice. A wave of fear crashed against the beaches of my consciousness and I was glad the bar remained solid, or I might have drowned.

Through a thick fog I said, "How?"

"He was by the door when you entered, Radshaw." Wilberford's mouth filled my vision, twisting into a smirk. "He left the moment he saw you didn't have the Angrath." The lower lip was plump and glistening with amused spittle. "He'll be at your office by now." The upper lip, despite encroaching moustache, was clear and delineated with sensitive grooves. "We have kept you long enough."

Suddenly all I could see was the back of my fist. I don't think I've ever hit someone so hard. The punch had all my shock, outrage, and a half hour's tuition with Lennox Lewis in 2002 behind it. Time moved like we were all trapped in treacle as my knuckles burst those bastard lips against Wilberford's teeth. Then I felt my bones crunch as they came up against enamel. My skin and his grin gave way simultaneously. I felt his lower jaw crumple and my blood mingle with his in a macabre cocktail and had time to wonder if I'd catch an infection.

Then the clock ticked and time returned with a crash of smashing bottles and folding shelves. He went down in a heap, and I was striding towards the door, phone in my good hand as the other dripped blood. A Knight approached between me and the exit, mouth opening to talk. I punched him with my ragged fist and he went down. As I pushed my way through the door into the night, uncaring if I was being chased, I clamped my phone to my ear.

Nobody answered.

*****

I crashed into my office with ears buzzing and roadrunner doing laps around my stomach. I'd already dialled 999 as I charged up the stairs; the claw marks on the door outside were all the reason I needed.

Broken furniture and shredded paper riddled the floor, but it was the slapdash strings of red that slammed my heart against my ribcage and held it in a chokehold. It looked like an expressionist painter had been flinging their brush around - lines smattered the windows, spattered the ceiling and matted the ground. All hell had broken loose in this place and everything was a mess.

The baby was not here. Even beyond my eyes and ears, I felt the lack of a presence I hadn't previously realised was there. Mr Black had the Angrath, but Amy hadn't made it easy.

"She fought!" I whispered to myself, my voice harsh through a closed throat. "She fought you, you fuck!"

There was a faint shuffle from behind my desk and I ran to investigate, torn between desperation to help and terror at what I might find. Amy was sprawled on her back, one foot stuck up on my overturned chair where she'd been hurled across the desk. Her body shuddered, her face was gone, and the whole world was slick with blood.

"Amy!" I roared, slamming to my knees beside her.

In response, a bubble popped in the pool where her features should be. There was a sound like a scream dunked in yoghurt and droplets splashed my face. Still breathing!

I grabbed her shoulder and pulled her onto one side, letting the blood drain from her mouth and nasal cavity. My fingers sank into a rent in her back and I quickly adjusted my grip. Tears rained from my face and mixed with her wounds.

"I'msosorry sosorry Amy. All my fault, so fucking sorry, that motherfucker! He's dead! I'll fucking ... oh god, I'm so fucking sorry!"

She glugged again and mucus spewed from a space that should have been her nose. What remained of her face was more visible now, and I thought I preferred the pool of blood. She tried to open her mouth, but it was already open. Too open. If I didn't do something, she'd be dead from blood loss long before the ambulance got here.

In a daze, I made sure she was balanced to her side and scrambled to my feet, trying to remember where the first aid kit was. I zigzagged round the room like a rubber bullet, bouncing between furniture and walls, my hands scrabbling at drawers and shelves for what I needed. Several breaths later, I stood over Amy's ragged form, an inch-long waterproof plaster gripped between thumb and forefinger, and sobbed listlessly. My brain arced from thought to thought so fast I felt like one of those lightning balls with jumping electricity in them.

Suddenly a clear thought broke through; a snippet of pop wisdom married to something I'd spied in a drawer. I scrambled to the place I'd seen it, frantic with haste, and soon I was back at Amy's side, a small tube of superglue in my shaking hand.

As I gripped the edge of a six-inch cut across her chest and drew the skin together, a resolve hit me. The shaking lessened and I knew I had to do this. If I did nothing, Amy would die. So even if superglue was the stupidest idea since someone decided The Matrix needed two sequels, it couldn't make things any worse. I squeezed some glue roughly along the broken edge of skin and pressed the gaping hole closed.

It held, and that gave me hope. I moved on, trying to decide which wounds to prioritise with a brain that thought triage had something to do with triangles. In one wound on her hip, I heaved and retched as I tied off a hanging tube that was dribbling a steady stream of blood into her intestines. Then I glued her shut. She made noises as I worked and I sniffed back tears, hoping with all my soul I wasn't torturing my only true friend unnecessarily. Within a few minutes, she looked, if not better, at least more human. Her chest still shuddered its way up and down, each breath accompanied by a hiss and more blood.

It was when I turned my attentions to her face that the shakes returned. She was making regular noises now, one hand nudging insistently as if trying to garner my notice. Unsure what was preventing her talking, I gently lifted open her mouth. Her tongue was attached but limp, sliced beneath by the same claw that tore her cheeks. At least her throat was intact, but a deep cut in the side of her neck, running on from her near-unhinged lower jaw, frightened the life out of me. That one needed fixing.

Steeling myself, I gently pulled the skin together with my fingers, and then applied a line of glue, holding the result in place. It wasn't until I moved my hands that I realised what my shaking fingers had done. As I pulled away, the side of Amy's face came with me. My hand, glued to the skin of her neck, peeled away her cheek, exposing gums and teeth. This time she managed a groan of distress and I choked back the vomit that rose on my palate. In desperation, I smoothed the skin back and held it with my other hand as I tore my stuck one free.

She jerked in place, moaning urgently, and I backed off in horror. Her head wobbled as it turned in my direction. Free from the pooled blood, all I could think was that she looked like an open doner kebab with way too much chilli sauce. One eye fixed on me from a mess of flesh and gristle.

"Ngo," she said. "Ngo, ake! Ogeesh, agheshk oo. Ngo!"

It was then I heard the sirens, beckoned by my panicked phone call, and understood what she was saying. *Go, Mike! Police arrest you. Go!*

"I can't. I won't!" I could heard my tone, pleading as though she controlled me. Deep down, I knew she was right, but I needed her to make that decision. She slumped back, apparently lacking the energy to talk any more, but that eye pinned me with an eagle's clarity.

I wanted my brain to shut down, my instincts to rule my reactions, but they were as much use as slate window panes right now. The sirens were getting louder and my tears were falling heavier. Amy's eye just stared, devoid of expression without a face to give it context, but I knew what she was saying. I could be a coward or a bastard, and I wanted neither option.

It was a memory that saved me, a memory of that case in the disused warehouse, the first time I'd encountered one of the demons' doors. I'd been beckoned by a baby's cry, my sense of bravery or stupidity drawing me into a nightmare of horror and madness. That baby had been beyond help, half formed into a grotesque approximation of life, and I'd broken its little head with my gun butt to end its suffering. Today, as my faithful Amy lay shredded and ruined upon the floor, there was another baby, perhaps not beyond my help. The coward begged me to stay and take whatever was thrown at me, to give up and let grief and fear rule my actions.

But the bastard knew I had to leave.

The gypsy woman had warned me I'd have to step into darkness before this case was out, and only now did I understand just how far that step would take me.

I met Amy's monocular gaze as my tears came to a halt.

"I won't let you down," whispered my mouth.

Then I turned and left her in a heap on the floor, so much clutter amongst the wreckage of my office, and wondered what the hell I was going to do.

CHAPTER 3 – PSYCHIC PSYCHOTIC

I strode through the back streets of Piccadilly Circus, my head spinning like a potter's wheel as my brain flopped around loosely on top. I wet my mental hands and tried to caress it back into shape, but my grip was flaccid and hesitant. I'd lost the baby I was meant to protect, burned a bridge with the Knights, got an old friend killed, and after the damage I'd seen and done to Amy's face ... No, that memory was like a barbed wire enema right now. Best stay focused on the case, and try to find the baby before Mr Black ended its frail existence.

Without another lead, it was all I could do not to head back to the Knights' seedy pub hideout and firebomb the shit out of it. Instead, I dialled the number they'd called from earlier and left a message:

"I'll deal with you later."

There was one upside to my situation; I had nothing left to lose. That was a bracing concept, and it hardened my thoughts like quick-dry cement. A man who loses everything has no fear and very little inhibition. A small part of me shrank from the clinical bent to my rationale, but if you're going to have a shitty experience, you may as well plumb it for wisdom.

The air wafted my hair and a lank lock tumbled across my face, dropping like a curtain before one eye. My head told me it didn't matter, that there were more important things to worry about than looking like a middle-aged rock fan with a goth complex. At that thought, I stopped dead in my tracks, right there in the middle of the pavement.

"Idiot," muttered a woman as she stumbled past, thrown off course by my unexpected halt. An idle corner of my brain conjured something horrifically rude in response, but it dissipated on the way to my mouth.

I pulled at the bandage round my knuckles, wincing as it aggravated the puckered tissue. That punch had been worth it, even more so in retrospect, but right now it hurt so much I thought even the dead would be able to feel it.

A light bulb turned on above my head - literally as well as figuratively, the electrics in the street lights doing the dance of bad workmanship. The dead feeling - there was a thought!

I made a very deliberate point of grabbing the lock of hair and brushing it back onto my head. As it moved, my vision cleared and the world got just a tiny bit brighter. In the wake of my hair's shadow, I caught something in my peripheral vision. An advertisement, dominating the window of a sad recession victim, was staring at me from a nest of notes saying 'Bill posters will be prosecuted'. Bill Posters was clearly in trouble, but the face on the advert didn't care. It was Vic Quantum, the people's psychic.

"What a cock," I mumbled to myself, but even as I spoke, a thought was forming in my head.

Vic Quantum was pointing at me from his own advert like the guy from the war posters with a huge moustache, except he was bald and raising one eyebrow so high Roger Moore would be suing if he caught sight of it. The ears had been photoshopped to near-Vulcan proportions and the eyes were impossibly blue. 'Are you dead?' demanded the advert. 'If so, I've got your number.' I winced - this guy was a prize muppet.

Nevertheless, he'd given me an idea. As shots went, it was longer than Dirk Diggler on a warm day. In a normal situation, when luxuries such as alternatives might exist, I'd have laughed and swept it under the carpet. But all my rugs had been pulled out from under me.

I was halfway through dialling Amy's number, ready to ask her to dig out Vic Quantum's address, when I remembered what had put me in this desperate position, the torn mess I'd left her in, the certain knowledge that she would never be pretty again. A tear tickled my face like a water fairy wearing her best feather outfit, but she was a clawed minx and left a terrible sting in her wake. In a numb haze, I utilised my phone's internet to do my own digging, and wondered if I would ever return to feeling normal.

*****

"Mr Quantum?" I growled into the intercom. I hated these things!

"No, I'm his receptionist." To call the speaker's voice 'camp' would be like naming a blue whale 'tadpole'. "Mr Quantum is in a very important seance."

"Not any more, he isn't. Let me in!" The recording studio was a plain metal door in a bright orange brick wall down one of Soho's many narrow side roads. I stamped my feet against the cold breeze and wondered if I'd been too aggressive, but anger was pulsing through my veins and I wanted to milk it before the inevitable descent into depression.

My voice must have carried something of the rawness welling inside me - or the receptionist was a complete wuss. Either way, a dull buzz sounded and I pushed my way through the door. The receptionist looked like Tim Curry in the Rocky Horror Show, if he'd spent a year in Ethiopia. He pointed through another doorway from his perch behind a desk, a sulky pout twisting his lips. I winked in response, and walked on through.

"Welcome, Mr Radshaw," said Vic Quantum. "I've been expecting you." He was sitting at a desk in a dark room, illuminated by a single light from above. His fingers were steepled beneath that ridiculous chin, a tribute to his own effigy as he rested elbows on the table. All around was a crowd of microphones and cameras, catching every conceivable angle.

I sat down in the chair placed conveniently opposite him. "A panicked update from your receptionist thirty seconds ago doesn't count as clairvoyance. Oh, and Roger Moore called - he wants his eyebrows back."

"Very droll," he said with a smile, "but hardly original. How can I help you? I can't imagine you're a believer, or did you just come here to hone your sarcasm?"

A vision flashed through my mind of rent flesh, blood trailing across skin in sticky streamers, of my friend shredded and mutilated by demon claws and teeth. I felt rather than saw my face drop towards the floor.

"Oh, I'm a believer, alright," I whispered, then

sprung my head up to match his sardonic gaze as steel slipped into my voice. "I just don't know if I believe in you."

"I'm good enough that my fame's spread, even across to the States. Can you claim anything like that?"

I smiled. "Only if you count my appearance as 'English guy eating burger in background' on episode forty six of Diners, Drive-Ins and Dives."

His eyes twinkled briefly as if in amusement. "What can I do to help you, Radshaw?"

"I'm in something deep, Quantum. A protection job - you don't want the details. I thought I could keep my charge safe, but it turns out I couldn't even protect my nearest and dearest. Now I got no leads, no charge, and no idea where to go next. I'm so fucked, my unborn children are feeling sore."

A smile twisted the corner of his mouth, but he didn't respond.

"If you can talk to the dead," I continued, "you just might manage to connect me to the one person who seemed to know what was going on. She's a particularly foul gypsy woman who recently got her insides turned into lawn ornaments, and she had something to tell me."

He nodded. "What is her name?"

"No idea. I just thought of her as 'she-woman dog type thing.'"

"I don't think I can call that over the ether without upsetting some spirits. How do you expect me to find her?"

I grinned, and it felt uncomfortable on my face. "I

don't think you'll need to look hard. I have a feeling she'll be waiting."

For the first time, Quantum looked uncertain. "I may not be able to help you, Mr Radshaw."

I felt my mouth relax as the grin disappeared. "What, just get too real for you? I got a missing baby, an impending apocalypse, and the only person I care about is in hospital with a face like a meat feast pizza. You think I give a fuck in the wind what makes you uncomfortable?" I leaned forward out of my chair until our noses almost touched. "Try."

"Okay," he said, blinking. "But please sit down, Radshaw. My security people are watching, and I pay them not to ask questions."

I nodded and thunked back into my seat. "Just wanted to be clear."

"You get this one for free, since you asked nicely. If you come back though, you pay the going rates."

I glared at him. "Take it out my royalties for appearing in your home videos."

He placed a candle in the middle of the table and lit the wick, then held his hands, palms up, either side. "Take my grasp, wrist to wrist."

I complied, suppressing the sarcastic comment that rose in my mind - this was too important. As mad as this idea was, I couldn't risk ruining it by alienating Quantum. Besides, there was always later.

"Watch the flame," he whispered, drawing out the 'a' unnecessarily. Then he lapsed into a susurrus of harsh, sibilant sounds.

"If you conjure up a snake, I'll go Potter on you," I

mumbled, but he ignored me and continued his diatribe. His wrists were cold in my grasp, and I could feel the tendons working beneath the skin despite his still hands clutched upon me. He was working some serious muscles further up the arms. All part of the show, I assumed. This was a guy who thrived on showing off, especially when he had a willing believer in his midst.

The flame reached into my gaze like a tongue hungry for eyeballs, dancing in sinuous motions; a snake beholden to its charmer. It curled and licked to the sounds of Quantum's shushing chant, a faint crackle tumbling through the air like excitement. It reminded me of my mad, stupid life. Always dancing to someone else's tune, hot with determination but ultimately just lighting the way for others to use me. In many ways-

"God, fuck my arsehole with a sandwich!" I roared, pulling back from the table. Quantum's head was flung back, mouth wide, screaming at the ceiling in a voice that made the girl in the exorcist seem timorous. His wrists were burning hot, searing at my palms, but I couldn't pull away. His fingers curled round my arms like constrictor snakes, binding me in place despite my motion. I crashed to my knees, stomach hitting the desk edge as my arms held me up. Getting a knee under, I pushed myself back into the chair as a wet cackle sounded. It was Quantum's vocal chords, but his voice had left the building.

I watched his head slump back into an upright position, his features so twisted it could have been a different face. Muscles quivered under the strain of yanking his mouth into a terrible grimace and his eyes were so wide they looked like evil ping-pong balls.

"What filling would you like, Radshaw?" rasped the face, harsh with guttural rawness. "God can't help you, but I might."

It was a moment before I understood what it was talking about. "On second thought, maybe I'll take an iced bun instead."

"Even in shock, you make jokes." A sound like a cat throwing up filled the room, and I realised it was a laugh. "Perhaps you should trying watching your organs arranged for decoration while you still live. Would you make jokes then?"

I blinked. "Repulsive gypsy crone, I presume."

The fixed mouth twitched; perhaps a smile. "Now deceased, but at your service, for a price."

"What?" I laughed despite myself. "I don't think Vic Quantum would thank me if he woke up to find I'd sprinkled blood and flob on him and wanked in his hand."

She chuckled. "Whilst your colourful image might be entertaining, you misunderstand. It's not the liquids I need - the medium is unimportant. I desire your lust, Mr Radshaw. Your pain and your vitriol; all those emotions you dare not admit. The dreams of rape, the rage-spiked desire to maim with bare hands. The darkness you deny so life is possible."

"Just tell me where Black went with the baby," I growled. "We have a score to settle."

"Cross my palm."

I contemplated head-butting her. It was irrational and wouldn't achieve anything beyond a moment's satisfaction, but the urge was strong nevertheless. Instead, I asked, "How?"

"Tell me your thoughts. The wicked ones - the things you can't admit."

I glanced around me at all the recording devices. "I have an audience."

She shrugged Quantum's shoulders. "That is your concern, not mine."

"When I was nine, my gym teacher humiliated me and I wished she was dead."

"Pathetic! All nine year-olds have such thoughts. They do not understand consequence. Only in a grown man's ire does true darkness reside. Tell me about dreams of fellating yourself with a girlfriend's severed head, of slicing the throats of all who wronged you."

I sighed. She wasn't going to let me off easy. "When I helped take down a street gang who were making kiddie porn to finance a demon excavation, I almost understood. I wondered if I'd have done the same things in their situation, and realised I might have."

She nodded. "Better, but evil done under duress is mitigated by diminished responsibility. Sate me, Mike. Let loose and tell me something really, horribly honest."

It was a while before I answered, but the thought had already been in my head - a thing I'd hid, even from myself, tied up in all the terrible shit I was dancing amongst. "I just had to glue my assistant's face back together 'cause a dirty fucking demon tore it up." I swallowed, recalling all the sensations I'd felt. "Each time she cried out because I tore her skin, or whimpered when I pulled too hard, I..." Snot clogged my throat and I sniffed expansively. "I felt a little rush inside. It felt like, well. It felt like a thrill." I looked straight into Vic Quantum's eyes, except they weren't his eyes. They were gleaming with lust for visceral emotion. "Some sick, sadistic part of me enjoyed inflicting the pain." I looked down again, and let the sobs take me.

A sigh wafted my hair from across the table. "Now we're getting somewhere, Mr Radshaw. Power is the greatest vice of man. The freedom to inflict pain on the helpless has seduced for millennia."

I stared hard at the table top in front of me, my brain seeking distraction in the details of the faux-wood grain. I followed a contour as it hugged the bullet hole of a knot.

"We always manage to abuse power," I said.

"Abuse is subject to interpretation. If you have power and use it, somebody will always see it as abuse. What you know, even if you won't admit it, is that power must be used. Otherwise, it's just a bomber without a pilot, sapping your resources without even trying to make a difference."

I smacked my hand down on the desk. "Are you going to help me, or do I have to listen to more metaphors?"

She sucked in a breath. "Tell me more. My palm is unfilled."

"No. I'm through plumbing the depths of my guilt so you can give this two-pence psychic a hardon. You want to help, otherwise you wouldn't have bothered coming. Give up the goods, or I'm gone."

The hands crunched even tighter on my wrists and fire slid along my bones. "Feed me, Radshaw. I need it!"

I glared directly at Quantum's eyes, wincing at the pain, anger flushing through my mind. An idea winked at me from the darkness of my thoughts, and I smiled. "I helped an elderly lady cross the road last week. I even carried her shopping."

"What are you doing? I don't want to hear this!"

"She'd bought cat food that was in an offer, but not got her second pack free, so I popped back to the shop for her and got the extra food."

She actually hissed, spreading Quantum's mouth even wider, if that was possible. "No! Stop this vile diatribe!"

I stood up, rearing over her even if I couldn't lift my hands from the table. "I love kittens! They're so cute and sweet. They make adorable little faces when they play. Kittens make me believe in the fundamental niceness of the world."

"Shut up! You will only undo your own designs."

"Sometimes, when I'm sad and lonely," I laughed. "I spend whole days talking to coma patients and volunteering in the children's ward. It doesn't make me happy, but I like to know that someone's life is benefiting from my efforts."

"Alright!" she stamped a foot for emphasis. "Okay, I give in. Please, leave me with the shred of negative I'm still clinging to. Sit down. I'll tell you what you need to know."

I did as she asked and settled once more opposite the form of Vic Quantum. The skin of his face and neck was looking strained and raw from the pressure of the expression she was pulling. He wouldn't be happy with me after this.

"Where can I find the Angwrath?" I whispered. "It's just a baby."

She sniggered. "Your ignorance is matched only by your predictability."

"So my first girlfriend kept saying, but hey, how was I meant to know where the clitoris was?"

"I like you, Radshaw. You have balls, and you aren't afraid to lay them on the butcher's block and hand him a meat tenderiser." Vic Quantum's face twitched, shifting in something like relaxation before she pulled it back into that heinous grimace. "Mr Quantum seeks to reoccupy his body, so we must conclude our business. The Angwrath may be a baby, but it is also a force for peace. It is the anti-wrath, a calming influence upon humanity. It births once in a millenium to placate the vicious tendencies of the population. So says the prophecy."

I leaned forward. "So Mr Black hates this thing - is that why he wanted it?"

"He is the demon of death. A calm population leaves him feeble."

"He wants to kill it," I sighed. "That means we're probably already too late."

"No, he wants to take it home."

"Why does that sound somehow worse?"

The face shifted again, and sweat glistened on the contended forehead. "The Angwrath is Angelspawn. It is more potent than you can imagine, and a power upon its environment. You will understand when you go there. Your only chance to avert the Black Dawn is to follow Black and retrieve that child. London cannot survive a new dark age."

"The Knights said angering him would bring the Black Dawn, that I was meddling."

"That is because they lack belief. You can open the doors, Radshaw, thanks to the taint they put in your hand. You can get to Black, and I can tell you which door to use. You must go now to have any chance."

I looked into those tortured eyes. "What if I fail?"

She grinned. "Then you and I shall have a picnic here in Hell, and lament the idiocy of man." With that, she told me where I needed to go, and I wondered if the world had shed its last vestige of sanity.

CHAPTER 4 – KEEPING AN EYE ON HELL

My hands felt like I'd been tossing off hedgehogs, and the bastards spunked acid. Quantum's grip, with its evil gypsy instigator, left raised welts stinging on my skin in the shape of his fingers. Still, the renowned psychic hadn't gotten off easy - I left him whimpering as he nursed blackened skin and fingers like pork scratchings. He told me channelling spirits sometimes left a mark on him, especially if they were violent or angry. Like mosquitoes, they deposited their psychic sewage while they were latched to him, leaving an irritating spot.

The old crone did the spirit equivalent of opening his head with a can opener, squeezing out a massive dump in his skull cavity, and reattaching his scalp with a staple gun.

I called St Thomas' hospital to ask about Amy's condition, but all they could tell me was she was in surgery. I hung up and walked, head hunched down against a London summer shower, towards the nearest underground station. The rain stank like sulphur and defeat - the vestiges of a dirtier age were whiffs on the air like ghosts of smog. For the first time in years, I felt utterly alone.

The weight of my gun made itself known from the shoulder holster under my coat. My only friend - a solid weight against the darkness - but about as trustworthy as a paedophile at a 1Direction concert. Giving guns to people seemed like sitting a child in front of a big red button marked 'global thermonuclear war' and telling them not to push it. Grant a man power and he'll find a reason to use it. One moment's chaos was all it took to steal a thousand tomorrows.

I smiled to myself, realising Amy would be telling me to snap out of it if she was around. The gun in my coat was probably the silliest garment since jeans that are actually designed not to fit round the arse, but I wouldn't be without it. Bullets did fuck-all to angry demons, but I'd been reared on a diet of Die Hard and Lethal Weapon, bred to believe firearms solved problems. In terms of my confidence, that felt true.

The rain caressed my face like a grease-caked glove on the hand of an inexperienced lover; warm, oily and grimier than a cat litter facial scrub. In a moment utterly against common sense, I was actually happy to get inside, even though 'inside' was a tube station. I jumped on the Circle Line - a metaphor for my life - and squeezed into a spot between armpits. It was approaching rush hour, so the trains were busier than Charlie Sheen's dealer, but the affected anonymity of a London crowd felt appropriate. The guy pressing close in front let out a fart like a nasal jackhammer then pretended not to notice. I laid my head on his shoulder and snuggled up, groaning appreciatively, knowing he had no space to escape. By the time I left the train at Embankment, he was sobbing softly, his gaze far away.

Mission accomplished.

I strode across the Thames on the bridge between Charing Cross station and the South Bank. The water lurked beneath me, lapping at its banks with intent. If the gypsy woman was right - and she had to be, because I had no other leads - I was almost at my destination. It turned ponderously through the skyline ahead of me, dominating the view.

The London Eye - designed to play second fiddle to the millennium dome, but it ended up conducting the orchestra. Who knew a poshed-up fairground attraction would come to define a city? As it turned out, the Eye was named more appropriately than anybody knew. It took forty eight minutes to turn a full rotation, which was exactly how long the elevator beneath it spent descending to the door into Mr Black's domain.

It's a lock, Mr Radshaw - a lock on the most important of all the doors. The Knights have tried to claim responsibility, but the London Eye was orchestrated at levels far beyond their understanding. Previously, access was only possible via a guarded tunnel from the bunker deep beneath Downing Street, but it seems even Prime Ministers can be too curious for their own good. Your hand will open Black's door, just as it does the other runed portals, but the entrance at the base of the Eye is guarded by entirely more human forces.

I studied the sensation roiling in my stomach as I walked. It felt like a bowling ball formed from snot, wire wool and a hundred bad curries, and my guts were not happy about it. It seemed like fear was my constant companion these days - not surprising when you've seen all the awful crap I get to deal with. It's come close to driving me insane once or twice. Hell, it might have succeeded - I mean, how would I know? Thing is, when you've got indigestion twenty-four-seven, it stops being debilitating and just integrates into your everyday reality. I was frightened like a lame dormouse in a nest of vipers, but the terror was just a tool on my utility belt.

"Suck it up, Mike. You can do this." I didn't talk to myself nearly as often as I used to, but without Amy's voice at the other end of a phone call, I needed to hear the words.

I descended the stairs to the bank and approached the base of the Eye, ignoring the absurdly long queue and heading down to one side. I passed the concrete base and threaded my way between giant metal supports, and then ran out of ground. *Funny - she didn't think to mention this.* The rear side of the foundation was actually out above the water of the Thames - a river so dirty, poo would swim upstream, salmon-like, to avoid being emptied into it. A description from a Terry Pratchett novel came to mind, of the river Ankh - the only river whose water could be collected with a net. I was pretty sure the Thames inspired that.

Still, there was nothing for it but to take the risk. Between falling in the Thames and a black apocalypse for all mankind, there was genuine debate to be hand, but I wasn't about to leave the baby to its fate.

I hugged one of the massive, white steel beams holding several hundred people up in the sky and swung myself out over thin air. My stomach lurched when my shoes failed to find any purchase, but I hung on grimly and resisted the urge to scramble. A glance back at the queue showed whole swathes of people managing to look in the opposite direction. City folk are adept in the art of not noticing anything that might cause complication or hassle. While I was distracting myself pondering the de-socialising effect of urban life, my sole found a crack between metal sections. It was just enough to get a corner of rubber into, so I inched my way round the support beam.

The water lapped hungrily beneath me. A glance at the back of the giant wheel showed me a shadowy alcove set into the concrete base, a few inches above the shifting river. It was designed to be invisible from almost any angle - unless you happened to be dangling from a metal support like a *fucking idiot.*

Creeping round the support until my back was to the alcove, I took two fast breaths and threw myself backwards. For the merest second, I thought I'd missed and envisioned being sucked beneath the water, a victim to the twin threats of surging currents and general skankiness. Then my heels struck solid ground and I crashed to my arse in the alcove, skittering into the shadows in case anyone happened to be watching.

Feeling my way round a corner, I found myself in complete darkness, deafened by the thunderous rumbling of gears and pulleys from inside. I lit up my phone to use as a light and studied what appeared to be a smooth concrete wall. A chuckle rose in my throat but I suppressed it, sensing the futility fuelling it.

My arsenal included an automatic handgun and a biting sense of sarcasm. If I had to break through a solid masonry block, they were about as much use as a marshmallow pickaxe. I briefly considered hurling some of my best insults at the wall - perhaps I could break down its confidence at a molecular level.

"Nah," I muttered, remembering playground confrontations. "That only works on people."

Another memory rose - of a street gang holding

me at gunpoint, trying to make me lead the way through an underground doorway for them. I shit myself that day - literally as well as figuratively. When you blindly put your hand through a portal and something shreds it, bowel control is suddenly way down on your list of priorities. My genuine horror in that moment - combined with shaking my suppurated digits in my captors' faces - saved my life. The encounter also left me with a demon-infused hand, able to open the secret portals dotted around London. It was an ugly hand, with skin so grey a zombie would be embarrassed and a terrible habit of giving people the finger.

Okay, so that last bit wasn't down to the demon taint.

Figuring I had nothing to lose, I raised that hand and gave the wall before me a solid middle finger salute. Once I was certain it'd got the message, I placed my palm flat against its surface and pressed gently.

Vibrations threaded through my fingers and drew lines of excitement along the edges of my bones. When the electric sensation reached my lungs, I breathed in a great gasp of air that felt like swarming bees in my chest. Yep, there was something dodgy about this wall, alright. That, or I'd unwittingly set up an insect sanctuary in my chest cavity.

The concrete shimmered and runes glowed black, showing up like clusters of spider legs crawling across my vision. Layers of grey shifted and swam until my stomach churned, darkening as the texture beneath my fingers altered. After a few moments, they settled into stillness and I found myself with a hand pressed against a timber door, its ancient, knotted surface rough and harsh beneath my skin. The runes were sunk into its surface, black as a pit in midnight's nadir. I was very glad I couldn't read them. This was more familiar territory - a creepy door leading somewhere I didn't want to go but went anyway.

With two deep breaths, I ignored that bole in my stomach that throbbed and scratched and told me to run, pushing on the demonic door. It creaked and gave way to the pressure, swinging ponderously away from me to reveal a room beyond. I wondered what I'd find - a slavering monstrosity, waiting to pluck my face from my skull; a black void ready to suck me into some terrible dark dimension; a group of knights who'd ambush me and dish out a good kicking.

Instead, I strode forward into a well-lit room that looked like a building entrance lobby. Two guards slouched behind a reception desk and a single elevator faced an entry door across the space in front of them. I'd come into the room behind the two guys, who were apparently oblivious to the groan of geriatric hinges I'd had to suffer. Realising they weren't aware of me, I stood stock still to eavesdrop, wondering what hideous demon's plans they might be discussing.

"I'm telling you, mate," one was saying. "She's got the best rack this side of the Dartford Tunnel. You gotta go a long way for fitter tits than them."

The other tutted as if in disgust. "Dude, it's all bra. Take it away and they'd be bouncing off her knees. Seriously - forget the rack. Always check out the arse. It's the only true measure of a fit bird."

"Arses are all well and good, but you can't bury

your face between them and do the jiggle shake."

"You could," laughed his companion, "but you might get hepatitis."

"You're sick, mate. I mean, what kind of nutter doesn't like big jugs?"

"Dude, I love jugs - just not hers."

I couldn't take any more of this. "Sorry to interrupt," I said, "but I don't think you should talk about Ann Widdicombe that way."

Jugs-Lover guy jumped six inches in the air and Arse-Man fell off his chair. "Who the fuck?" shouted the jumpy one, now on his feet, fumbling inside his jacket.

I had about five seconds to contain this before their wits returned and they set about perforating me. "I need to get through here," I said, flashing my ancient, long-outdated police warrant card for exactly one tenth of a second.

Jugs-Lover opened his mouth to speak again, so I cut him off.

"The name's Radshaw - Supernatural Affairs. That's a department, not an internet dating service. You have to let me through, or it'll be curtains."

"Curtains?"

I nodded. "Velvet, with lace filigree and blackout lining."

"What?"

"Exactly."

"Hang on a minute." Jugs-Lover held up a finger.

I didn't give him a chance to continue. "Look, I'm not making this up."

"Eh?"

"Seriously - some people actually say 'it'll be curtains' and I can't explain it. Now, which one of you is going to accompany me?" I strode past them while they shared uncertain glances, heading for the elevator. "Come along, one of you. We can't keep 'his highness' waiting now, can we?"

"You got clearance?" asked Arse-Man, heading over. His gun was out but he held it casually at his side - I wasn't currently a threat.

"Code Alpha, Level 6, Spectrum Priority," I said, hoping my eyes didn't look as manic as my brain felt. "The nail on my big toe outranks you, son. Now get this door open."

He pulled keys from his belt and slid a chunky one into a hole by the lift doors. He slumped slightly before turning it, looking at me. "I never actually opened this before. The bossman always does it himself. He said we should keep our eyes open."

"Quite right."

He turned the key and the doors parted with that subtle swish only the most mind-numbingly expensive technology manages to make. I strode into the bright silver interior with a lion's presence and a rabbit's confidence. Thankfully, Arse-Man followed me in without my needing to speak - I didn't trust my voice right then.

The panel held only one button, and it was entirely red. I was mildly surprised not to see a glowing skull in its centre. In my mind, a sign underneath it read 'Heart of Darkness' but my mind was unreliable right now.

"Off to see Mr Brando's head," I muttered, and

pressed the red dot with my thumb.

The dampers were good, because I barely sensed movement, but my feet felt instantly lighter - this thing was going down faster than a Thai stripper with a green card in her eyes.

"What's going on here?" said Arse-Man uncertainly.

I turned and kneed him in the bollocks as hard as I could, then retrieved his gun as he slumped, gagging, to the floor.

"Your unlucky day, mate," I said. "Sorry about that. Problem is, you have things a bit backwards. The bossman, as you call him, is the guy you're here to keep in. Sounds to me like you let him come and go as he pleases. And that," I nudged him with a toe, "is bad for your balls."

He groaned and dribbled, but managed to speak. "Mr Black's not normal, dude. He's a proper mean, scary motherfucker. You know how fucked you are right now?"

"Oh, I've been fucked, impregnated, given birth and watched the devil grow into a seriously disturbing doppelganger. There's no hope for me, mate. I lost the battle long ago. I'm here for other reasons." I matched the guy's hurt gaze and shrugged, cocking his gun for effect.

"I got a score to settle."

CHAPTER 5 – PISSING IN THE TIGER'S MOUTH

The elevator penetrated Earth's defences, dropping with the inevitability of death into a hole I wasn't sure I'd climb out of. I felt like an eighteen year-old virgin invited to Hugh Hefner's mansion. My eyes were eager but I wasn't very bright, and I left my chastity belt at home.

I pulled my long coat tighter and cleared my throat. If *that* was what Mr Black wanted, he'd have a fight on his hands.

"Why are you doing this?" said the prostrate security guard from the floor of the elevator. He'd carefully positioned himself so my foot couldn't easily connect with his balls. I didn't blame the man.

I smiled. "I'm sure my psychotherapist and I would give different answers, but I'm doing this because a childhood trauma left me with unresolved daddy issues. My only answer for the rage I never got to express is to throw myself into hopeless situations. Trouble is, I'm also determined not to die, because I don't have a death-wish, you see, just an abiding need to beat death at every opportunity, even if that means goading him."

He didn't respond but his expression was talking, and it was saying three dots in a row or (in text language) 'wtf?'

"Glad you asked. Actually, that was my therapist's answer. Could you tell?" I squatted down next to him so I could lean my face right into his. "I'm doing this because some evil cunt who thinks he can run about doing whatever he likes kidnapped a baby and took it somewhere properly fucked up. Sure, it's an Angwrath or an angel's son or something, and I'm sure I don't understand it. It's still a baby, though, and last time I checked, that's not okay."

My expression must have conveyed how serious I was, because a tear escaped one of the guy's eyelids. "I just do my job, I swear. I get paid to sit in that room and not ask questions. I never knew who was meant to go in or out. I just know the bossman comes and goes most days."

"Thanks to you, he's been popping out for his daily walks, where he intimidates knights, separates actors down the middle and turns my loved ones into tagliatelle."

"I didn't know, man - I just follow orders."

I stood up so I didn't head-butt him. "You don't want to be using the Nazi defence with me, mate. I'm this close to gagging you with your own intestines."

"You got anger issues, man."

I snorted. "We all need our coping mechanisms."

The lift kept on plunging. Just how deep was this door into Mr Black's domain? Forty Eight minutes at this speed was an immense distance. *To the centre of the Earth and beyond,* supplied my unconscious. A few years ago, I'd have asked myself what was more central than the core of the Earth. These days I knew better. Sometimes, answers are worse than a thousand unrequited queries.

*****

The doors swished open like well-oiled curtains. Instead

of sunlight pouring in, they admitted a meaty fist with a blond crew-cut peeping over the top. It might have caught me smack in the face, but I'd come prepared.

Arse-Man, who had the misfortune of being my human shield, took the punch square on the nose. He went down like a sack of rotting potatoes and I threw my own punch across his toppling head.

Sir Wilberford was standing in the lift doorway, an expression of triumph on his face. "Got you back, Rad-" he said before he realised his mistake. I watched his face go from jubilant to a sort of pouty resignation when he saw my knuckles approaching. "Oh, fu-"

My fist crashed into his purple, misshapen jaw like a bag of stones striking over-ripe blueberries. Blood spurted from his mouth and spattered away from my freshly ruptured hand. He staggered back, hands clasping his face, squealing in muffled agony. I stepped over my unconscious human shield and shoved Wilberford to the ground, shaking blood from my damaged fist. It hurt like a cactus butt plug but the pain was worth it.

"You really ought to get that face looked at," I said. He moved his hands away from his jaw to brace himself on the floor and glare at me. I sucked in a breath. "On second thought, nobody should have to look at that. Your mouth looks like you lost a fight with a lawnmower."

"kyou," he managed, getting his message across despite a lower jaw that wasn't connected properly any more.

"I was hoping I'd meet you again, Crunchy Nut." I planted a boot in his gonads to make sure he wouldn't get up anytime soon. "You know what Black did to my assistant when he took the baby? If you ever looked at the blades on a cross-cut shredder and wondered what your hand would look like after going through there..." I leaned forward across his form to look directly down into those bright blue eyes. "That's a small part of how her face looked."

We matched gazes, eyeball to eyeball, until he spat to one side and glared up at me again. Apparently, that was all the answer I was getting.

"My heart feels like a barbed wire jumping bean right now," I said. "That's anger, Wilberford - more anger than most guys feel at one single time - and you're the cause. It hurts so bad, I feel like the only way to get rid of it would be to punch your idiot face till it sticks backwards from the rear of your head."

I made to slam my bleeding fist down into his face and he flinched, turning aside, his eye twitching like a dying mosquito. "That's better," I whispered. "That's the state of mind you deserve to be in, Wilberford. But you know what? I'm not gonna kill you. I'm gonna let you bleed and ache and suffer till you feel a small part of the hopelessness you've caused me - and no doubt others. The Knights might have been dickheads before, but at least they knew what was right. You turned misguided knowledge into wilful ignorance, and that's just fucking retarded.

"I can't explain to you just how wrong you are, because you're the kind of shit-farmer that thinks belief is more important than facts. Instead, I'll let you breathe, and every breath can taste of defeat, because that's what this is. I have power over you, Wilberford -

the power to decide your fate, the power of life or death. And you? You're a fart in a blossom tornado. Remember that while I try to save the city you helped put in danger."

His glare was turning watery as I looked away, finally able to take a glance at where the lift took me. A far cry from the office building lobby at the top, this was a dark cave with flaming sconces for illumination. Swathes of orange light moved around the space like clouds in a hurricane, highlighting the naturally craggy rock walls in alternating fire and shadow. The small alcove I'd walked into funnelled into a corridor ahead. Apart from the acrid crackle of the naked flames, the air vibrated with muffled clanks and whirrs from above. An underlying stink of sulphur and burning flesh lurked on the air's undercurrents.

If Satan dropped his shorts, bent over and hung a sign on his back saying 'this way to paradise,' that would be more welcoming.

Still, I'd been cut beyond the point of normal tolerance on this case, and some bastard kept pissing on the wounds. I wasn't about to be stopped by a creepy corridor.

"Here, blacky blacky blacky," I mumbled as I walked forward, then stopped myself when I realised I sounded like an extra from Mississippi Burning. I was in enough trouble without upsetting any pressure groups. Light flickered ahead like an intermittent strobe, but the darkness didn't last long. Only a few steps into the corridor, I encountered a door. No, scratch that. This was definitely a **Door** - as openings went, it was a prince among portals, and thoroughly worthy of the capital letter.

Firelight clung to the gilded frame as though burning from within. Intricate details threaded their way through the gold outline, delicate and fine but as clear as Arial Bold on a white background. The glimmering metal outlined the oldest-looking door I'd ever set eyes on. What looked like oak so ancient it'd seen the rise and fall of ideologies filled the space with implacable timber. The runes crowding its surface were stark and deeply set, sucking shadow and seething with black fervour. On closer inspection, I saw each was a larger, mirrored version of a corresponding shape on the gold frame.

This was something new, or possibly older than I could imagine. All the demonic doors I'd encountered seemed impregnated with an eerie life force, but this one positively pulsed, its shape shifting, bulging and retracting as I gazed at it. The gypsy called it the most important of all the doors, and its design certainly supported that description.

I hesitated in front of the wood, uncertain. My tainted hand opened all the other doors, but the metal reflections here indicated a type of security, and I didn't want to know what kind of measures that might imply. A particularly bold line of runes across the top suggested some form of warning. A Nightwish song came to mind as I cast my eyes across their sinuous designs. *Is this the end of all hope?*

"You don't read demon, Mike," I said, sighing, and placed my grey hand firmly against the portal.

The grain was clearly delineated against my skin's touch, rough but suffused with an inner warmth. A sting pressed into my palm where it covered runes but I ignored it and pressed harder. The sigils around the edge lit up in black light. I know, I know - that sounds like a contradiction. Imagine shadows glimmering, black lens flares spearing in your vision as the darkness pulses. If you can do that, you're some way towards seeing what I did. Pain lanced into my skin like barbed hooks, latching my flesh to the channels of the timber. It might be designed to make me pull away in response, but I don't much like that hand anyway.

I pushed with all my might, bracing my other hand to the first one's elbow and my feet against the ground with bent knees. As I focused my every muscle on the task, shoving for all I was worth, my reward was grudging movement. At first, I thought my feet were just sliding away under the force, but the grinding vibrations - along with the appalling stench emanating from the crack - made me realise the door was opening.

The runes jittered and sparked, making noises like popping candy on a tongue. With a little more motivation, I thought they'd be attacking me in a bee-like swarm. The smell hit me like a face full of rotting kippers, a near-physical presence in the air ahead. I bit down on the gag pushing my throat towards my teeth and snorted out a hard, snotty breath as I strained every ounce of strength, barging the door all the way open.

I fell in when it moved, falling flat on my face on what felt like a plush, shagpile carpet. It smelled like flowers, which seemed deeply wrong. I mean, flowers are nice and all, but a floral carpet in a demon's dimension is like a smile on a constipated dictator. My brain just wouldn't let me trust it.

The door screeched and grumbled as it shifted closed and I rolled out of its way. I found myself looking up at an immaculately detailed ceiling, every inch covered by a breathtakingly painted scene. For a moment I thought it was the Sistine Chapel, until I noticed where most of the fingers ended up.

"Trust a demon to turn good art into perversion," I muttered.

"I can assure you, good sir," said a voice in that ridiculously posh English accent only used by royalty and piss-takers, "this is very much an original. Michelangelo painted this first, between 1503 and 1507, to explore the concepts of philosophical insights as represented by digital penetration. He painted over it for public consumption, of course, but not before Mr Black captured its beauty for his home."

I craned my neck, feeling the impossibly soft carpet caressing my hair, to look up at the man standing by my head. As I'd suspected, he was dressed as an English butler. If he was any more stereotypical, he'd be running the equal opportunities committee for Greenwich County Council. The formal attire was immaculate, the chest puffed proudly outwards, and I had way to good a view straight up his impressive nose.

"Greetings, Mister Radshaw. Your arrival is not entirely unexpected."

I blinked. "You need some WD40 for your front door. If it was any harder to open, people would call it the ketchup bottle last used by Geoff Capes. You know - back when he was world's strongest man and rolled minis over and stuff." I blinked again. "I mean, not now, 'cause he'll be properly old. Or possibly dead - is he dead? I'll have to check Wikipedia."

The butler didn't bat an eyelid. "I shall have to see to the door at my earliest convenience. The master passes directly through it, you see. You are the first person to actually open it in, by my estimation, nine hundred and seventy three years." He fished in a breast pocket for a tiny note. "Mr Black bade me tell you, should you, indeed, appear ... ahem," He squinted at the note. "*Fuck you Radshaw, you come-guzzling scrote.* Forgive me, he was explicit in his instructions that I should read the message exactly as he penned it. *If you come for me, you'll be deader than Ghandi's flip flops in the height of summer. The Angwrath's mine, it's staying mine, and it'll be mine forever.* I believe he stole that phrasing from a Hula Hoops advertisement. Anyway, there is a little more. *Keep away, or I'll send you to Sodom's domain. Yeah - he's a demon too. One day I'll tell you about the real four horsemen. He likes visitors, but they don't like him.*"

I wiped snot from my upper lip. "That's it - those are his best shots?"

"I do apologise for the profanity, Mister Radshaw." He tucked the note back in his pocket. "My master is usually more eloquent, but he tells me he has been learning from the best."

"He has a way to go." I climbed to my feet and was happy to note I was taller than the butler. We were in a long hall with pristine white dining tables set out along both sides. Behind me was a glass-paned door that looked nothing like the reality I knew hid behind it, and at the other end of the hall was a an arch with what looked like a sunlit lawn beyond. From some where non-specific, a blanket of light was being cast.

I poked the butler in the centre of his chest. "You tell Mr Pink, or whatever his name is, if he's done anything to hurt that baby, I'm going to shove my arm so far down his throat I can grab his ring-piece and pull him inside out. Then, when he looks like an out-take from The Fly - we're talking Cronenberg, not Neumann - I'll hang him in the back of my toilet bowl like one of those pee-freshener things, and piss on him for the rest of my natural life."

To my satisfaction, the butler's eyes actually widened - almost a histrionic reaction, based on his otherwise stoic demeanour. "I believe sir is correct - my master does indeed have a way to go. I shall convey your colourful and physiologically unlikely message to him at once. When you hear thunder, you can be sure the missive has been delivered."

I watched him pootle away like a giant penguin. I'd made it this far, descended to a whole new layer of hell. And now I found myself in what looked like the inside of a wedding pavilion. I didn't know what I'd been expecting, but this wasn't it. I mopped a sheen of sweat from my brow.

"What kind of fucked up dimension is this?"

CHAPTER 6 – SUGARLAND SAGA

Home is where the heart is, I thought as I surveyed my surroundings. If that was true, Mr Black's heart must be a ball of candyfloss in a green field, surrounded by rabbits and flowers.

Somehow, that was more disturbing than the black fear and violence I'd envisioned.

A breeze tousled my hair like a playful lover, carrying with it the smell of fresh-baked cookies and aromatic roses. It sent shimmers across the immaculately tended lawn before me, filling the distance between the pavilion I'd arrived in and a hedgerow maze. Beyond the maze, everything was obscured by a grey pall, but right here the sun lit up the landscape like a thousand floodlights, saturating colours and soaking everything in comfortable warmth.

I wondered idly if the butler had to traverse the maze every time he travelled through the garden. Something told me he knew a few shortcuts. I strode forward beneath a sky so blue it looked like cartoon characters could drown in it. Whatever I might find or accomplish here, it was obvious I'd have to get through the maze first - something I found both twee and deeply irritating. I mean, as a device to slow down your enemies, it's not exactly original or fitting, is it?

Sighing sarcastically in the hope someone might hear, I plunged into the maze.

After an hour of walking with one hand brushing the left hedge, I came to the conclusion the maze was cheating. My hand looked like an inflated rubbed glove with a skin condition - some git filled the maze's hedges with stinging nettles.

I'd been hearing occasional rustling from behind me. Initially, I'd assumed it was the wind until I realised there was no breeze blowing when most of the sounds issued. Something was following me, trying to be sneaky. If it was that stereotype pastiche butler, he'd get a hiding like he'd never imagined. I felt the anger rising like a tide through my guts. I'd come here to get things done - to rescue the Angwrath and show that tosser Mr Black why he shouldn't have messed with Amy. Getting lost in a stupid, cheating maze wasn't part of the plan, and every moment wasted felt like swallowing a hedgehog.

When the noise sounded again, tentative and clumsy, the anger bubbled into my brain.

"For fuck's sake, you're not being subtle! You'd better show yourself, or I'm going to open up such a can of whoop-arse, you'll think harpies are nestling in your skull. Do it - face me or *fuck off*."

A shadow rose over my silhouette on the ground, casting its shape from behind. I couldn't turn to face the caster because I was busy watching horns emerge from my head as another shape overtook mine. *Oh, bollocks.* All at once, my head was conjuring up its myths and legends. I was in a maze, and it was a pretty mystical maze. It was here to guard a great evil. What creature does one expect to find in such a place?

"Hello, Wadshaw," said a gruff voice. Two things struck me. First, it didn't sound like a naturally deep voice - more like a child trying to sound grown up. Second, as ominous opening lines went, 'Hello, Wadshaw' was about as scary as Jonathan Ross in a pink tutu.

I turned around and immediately fought a laugh. I lost.

The creature before me put cute hands on cute hips, further accentuating his general cuteness. "Now see, that's just wude."

Okay, so let me paint you a picture here. He's a minotaur, right? So take that as your base image, then shrink it to three feet tall (if it was already three feet tall in your mind, there's nothing I can do for you). Now let me add some details. Candy floss hair, waving like a performing poodle-rocker. A polo through his bull's nose, making me shudder at the thought of mint in my sinuses. Ice cream cone horns - yes, seriously; they even looked stuck on with actual ice cream. A chocolate fake tan covered most of his visible skin but lick marks showed on his arms. Thankfully, he was wearing a teeny loincloth, allowing me one mystery I was happy to leave unsolved, but it was his nipples that really drew my attention.

They were fruit pastilles.

"I know what you're thinking, so please stop." Even with his high voice, he sounded weary and fed up.

I shrugged, just about containing my laughter. "What?"

"You're thinking *can I put one in my mouth without chewing?* The answer's no you can't - and no, you can't."

I sniggered - I just couldn't help it. "It's a shame they're not green ones - nobody likes those."

He scowled down at me from his position on the top of the hedge. "Come on, get it out of your system. I know there's more."

"Dude, you're pink."

"If only I had her singing voice." He shrugged his proportionately gigantic shoulders, dislodging a sprinkling of popping candy.

"No, I mean-"

He growled but it sounded more like a cat's purr. "I know what you mean. You think I chose this colour?"

I smiled. "I really needed that moment of levity, mate, so you've done me a great favour. I'm wondering if you can do me another one."

He jumped nimbly to the ground. "You want me to lead you out of the maze."

I nodded.

"I can help you, as long as you pwomise not to eat me." He reached up a hand in offering.

"Not a sentence I expect to ever hear again." I took his hand, and we plunged ahead into rumbling thunder and encroaching grey.

*****

A short while later, we were in a different part of the maze and I was absently licking my sticky hand. When I caught the mini-minotaur glaring at me, I wiped it on my trousers and took his hand again. He was adamant we needed to maintain physical contact to get me out of the maze. It didn't help that he hadn't stopped bitching since we set off.

He sighed. "The weal twagedy's downstairs - twust me."

"Do I want to know what it's made of, beyond something sweet?"

"Exactly what it is ain't the problem." He looked up at me and I looked into his anguished eyes. "Imagine being the guy evewyone offers blow jobs - you got something hanging off you chicks actually want to put in their mouths."

I smiled. "I can see how that would be an advantage, yeah."

"You'd think." He scowled. "Believe me, it felt amazing that first time. There I am, laying back while a flower-petal Miss Bo Peep does the business, and after a few sugar-sywupy minutes, I get welease and she gets pudding."

"So far, so..." I winced. "Sticky."

He nodded. "Pwoblem is, laying back afterwards, I notice a lightening of the load. I look down, only to see my piece's shrunk! That's not cool."

"Ahh," understand dawned over me. "So, it's like a gobstopper - keep sucking and you keep getting flavour, but eventually it withers away." I paused. "Well, if nothing else comes of this mad excursion, I'll never be tempted by gobstoppers again."

He sighed. "I wouldn't call it a gobstopper any more, more like a half-melted Malteser."

"Strike them off the list, too. Seriously, can we talk about something else?

"Such as?"

"Such as why the demon of death populates his domain with sunlit fields and sweet-shop mythical beasts."

He sneezed, then offered me the hand he'd put over his nose. "Want some gum?"

"No, and stop avoiding the question."

"We're not supposed to talk about it, on pain of ... well, pain."

I stopped walking, forcing him to a halt. "So you do know what's going on."

"Nope." He pursed his lips and shook his head, wafting the sticky scent of candy floss into the air.

"If you don't tell me, I'll eat you, starting with your toes and working my way up. Then, when the only bit left is Little Bo Peep's leftovers - 'cause I ain't putting *that* in my mouth - I'll auction it off on ebay."

He stared at me for a few moments. "Man knows how to bargain. Okay, I'll tell you how it is."

I nodded and we start walking again. "Are we nearly out of this bloody maze?"

"A few more minutes and we'll be clear. So, here's how it is. This place used to be a black nightmare, filled with tewain that made Mount Doom look like a marshmallow cat-nipple. Clouds of dwy acid swarmed through the air like angwy hornets and shadows without light sources slunk through the deep voids of blackness. I was a dark flame back then, spweading my anti-illumination, a pall of grim tastelessness and humour's dearth."

"Like Jim Davidson."

"Then, a few centuwies ago, it all started to change. From nowhere, there was light and all us occupants were burned away, leaving us floating like ghosts on the wind. We watched the dawning of colour, washing over our beloved hell like a sea of giggling children drowning out a great death metal tune. The air turned sweet, wivers of wancid magma turned to caramel and what once threatened ... beckoned. Worst of all, he brought us all back as new beings, wediwecting our essences into howifying yummy bodies like the one I'm forced to inhabit.

"That was when we wealised the Master was bwinging the Angwath here. You see, it's more than just angelspawn - the Angwath is a creature of both light and dark, product of a union twixt angel and demon, heaven and hell. An ancient agreement between Her upstairs and Him below makes sure two - usually unwilling - participants meet once evewy millennium or so. They get with the sweaty and the wesult is an Angwrath."

"Please don't use the word 'twixt' again." I grimaced. "It makes me think about Twix bars, and I don't want to think about eating sweets when I'm holding one's hand."

"And there I was thinking it was 'get with the sweaty' you'd object to."

"That was next on my list. Can I just ask?" I dragged him to a halt again. "You seem to have inherited my penchant for overblown analogies - is that intentional?"

He shrugged. "Yeah, I can't help that. I'm a mental being - by which I mean I'm constructed of thought processes, not bonkers. My name's Azza, which would mean more to you if you knew your theological lore."

I raised my eyebrows and he chuckled.

"My name means 'the strong' - my angel name. When I fell, I was stwipped of all native physical form, left only my thoughts without the chemical restrictors of a body. As a result, I pick up the conceptual essences of entities near me. Effectively, I'm starting to talk and act like you because of our proximity. It's probably why I'm helping you - I followed you long enough for your underlying sense of nobility to infect my consciousness. There was your threat of torture too, of course."

I snorted. "Great, now I'm an infectious disease as well as a pain in the arse."

"Don't talk to me about pains in the arse. This one time-"

"Nope." I dragged him into motion again to cut off his sentence. "I'm ninety eight percent sure I don't want to hear the rest of that sentence. You have at least explained why you've started pronouncing more of your Rs, which is a relief - you were a little too cute with that impediment. So come on - the Angwrath is a product of celestial entities bonking, a product of both heaven and hell. What does that mean for the baby?"

"It means it goes both ways." I threw him a scowl and he smiled wryly. "The purpose of an Angwrath is to create balance. That's why the powers that be agreed to a regular timeframe of a thousandish years. Most humans believe it will be a force for good, improving the world as it grows and lives - you know, like that Jesus kid."

"Seriously?"

"Oh yeah - no bull." He chuckled when I stared down at him. "Sorry, couldn't resist."

I shook my head. "A mad old gypsy lady told me

the Angwrath was a calming influence on the populace, designed to chill things out. I'm not sure 'that Jesus kid' really calmed things down. She said Angwrath meant anti-wrath."

"No, ang is the ancient word for tranquillity, and wrath hasn't changed. An Angwrath is literally a good-bad. Trust humans to misinterpret *everything*. Jesus turned into a force for improvement because the world was pretty damned shitty at the time. Entities like Mr Black - actually, you should think of him as Abaddon, that might help you if you face him - were in their ascendance, so the Angwrath's nature drove his powers to lessen theirs. The same would have happened in the 1040s, but Abaddon and a posse of fellow dark demons - the four horsemen - mounted a raid and killed the child in her first few days of life, when she was still vulnerable. That caused all kinds of unrest, and ended up changing the political make-up of England drastically."

I rolled my hand. "So how does this lead to the sugarland saga level we're walking through - why didn't they just try to kill this baby too?"

The pink mini-minotaur grimaced. "This time, he's got an even eviller plan. Yeah, I said eviller - it's a word because I say so. A few decades ago, Mr Black realised the world was heading down the poop chute of destiny, and the next Angwrath would change that if it was allowed to develop. So he turned his pocket-hell - the lovely land we're currently traversing - into the most lovely, blissful, sickly-sweet place imaginable. Now he's brought the Angwrath here, where everything is overbalanced towards beauty and justice and everyone gets everything they want."

"Except an unshrinkable penis."

"Well, there are always exceptions."

I sighed. "Sorry, I still don't get it. What's the point?"

"You really are a fucktard, aren't you?"

"Oi!"

"Hey, it's your word, Wadshaw. I picked if from your thoughts."

"One of this generation's few worthwhile inventions," I nodded. "And don't think I don't know that last W was intentional.

"The point," said my miniature guide, chuckling, "is the Angwrath, in such an unbalanced environment, will grow to create balance. It'll turn things here bad, at least enough to even things out. Black's plan is to bring it up in such a good place that everything it's driven to do will be evil. Then, once it's a teenager and its powers formed..."

"He'll unleash it back on Earth," I finished.

"Exactly. Oh, and just to warn you, it's probably about ten by now. You know, thanks to inter-dimensional time dilations and all that guff."

"Of course. We wouldn't want it to be easy or anything, would we?" The end of the maze loomed ahead - an arch carved from hedgerow. I heaved a great sigh of relief. Finally I felt like I was making progress. "And just how much damage can this Angwrath do, in that situation?"

"Imagine the new testament, but inverted. Plentiful food turned to a single fish, wine turned to water," he shuddered, "the rewarding of evil deeds, the lauding of debauchery."

"So, not all bad," I snorted.

He smiled and it didn't have an ounce of humour in it. "Or, if you'd like a visual representation..." He paused and beckoned through the arch. I stepped into the gap and stopped, stunned, staring at the roiling vista before me.

"Fuck my arse with a jackhammer."

The sugar creature's chuckle was sarcastic when it drifted to my ears. "If you're determined to carry on, Radshaw, you should be careful what you wish for."

CHAPTER 7 – TO KILL A MOCKING RADSHAW

My foot crunched down like a lunar landing vessel, sending up wafts of disturbed ash. *This is more like it.* I strode ahead into the sea of grey flakes, aiming myself at the pillar of rock I could see in the distance. Before he waved goodbye at the maze's exit, Azza told me that was where I should head. When asked a final time why he was helping me, he shrugged and said he was punishing Abaddon for rendering him in sugar.

A dull ache was emanating from my scratched hand. It felt bone-deep, like the marrow in my forearm was made of molten marshmallow and it was eating away my skeleton from the inside. It'd bothered me in the past, but nothing like this. Who knew, perhaps my marrow was considered evil, and it really had been turned into glycerine.

Thunder cracked overhead like a whip snapping against heaven, wielded by the fifty foot woman. Swathes of fire licked at the clouds with infernal hunger. Judging by the state of the ground, if it started to rain I'd need rock-based shelter or a Teflon scalp. Shards of landscape were thrusting up at the sky from the beleaguered earth, although a closer look suggested they'd speared into it from above.

On balance, I amended my previous thought. If it started to rain, I'd need an undertaker.

"As first visits to hell go," I mumbled, "this has certainly made an impression."

The storm seemed centred around the pillar of rock, and it was a reasonable guess the Angrwath was there. It was spreading, the roiling clouds expanding away from their source in concentric circles like water disturbed by a pebble. No - not extreme enough. More like a lake when a meteorite's just hammered into it. Soon, the sickly sweet maze would be corrupted into filth and terror, and Azza would become something I *really* didn't want to meet.

Travelling the bleak landscape, I found myself longing for the urban dirt of London. There were times I hated that shithole, and most of those times happened in the last few days, but at least it was *my* shithole. The air here wafted against my face like a thousand dog farts and there was nothing I could do to escape.

My ankle wobbled under my weight and I only just rescued it. Fatigue was taking its toll. Adrenalin and crappy experiences would only keep me going so long, but I knew I had to make it. Even if I failed, I needed to confront the bastard who caused all this misery - even if all I managed was to mildly irritate him. Even if he paused to kill me and that delayed his plans by a few moments.

Sometimes, the 'even if's are all we have. Sometimes, the act of defiance itself is all that matters.

I thought about the Knights, and Wilberford's belief Black should be allowed to continue because it was his 'turn.' What a numpty. That made about as much sense as sitting on a spike because you already have diarrhoea. The Knights weren't all bad, but their need for strong leadership was a serious weakness.

"I should have killed him." As a thought, it was logical, and I've never believed in heroes, but there are things your mind doesn't let you do. Killing a guy whose face I've already mangled while he writhes on the floor happens to be one of them. Perhaps that's all there is to human behaviour - what you do and what you don't - and the consequences arising from it.

I shook my hand as it throbbed again, the sensation travelling up my arm like a flow of nausea. It might just have been the light, but I was sure it looked more pallid than usual. In fact, it had that Night-of-the-Living-Dead look - and I mean the black and white version, here. There was probably a name for the condition, and that name likely began with 'necro.'

It felt like several hours later when I arrived at the rock tower and faced the unrivalled joy of climbing hundreds of steps. I climbed the first one out of sheer bloody-mindedness before sitting on the next one. My throat felt drier than a Jimmy Carr one-liner but I didn't have anything to drink. A rummage in my pockets - usually something I wouldn't risk, but desperate times and all that - yielded a boiled sweet between four and ten years old. It looked like a cross between cat poo and a seriously mouldy new potato, the wrapper engulfed in grey fluff. I studied it for a while, imagining the things I'd rather eat. Susan Boyle's g-string, for example, or my own underused testicles.

All at once, I wasn't so desperate after all. I dropped the 'sweet' back in my pocket, wiped my hand, and set off climbing the staircase.

*****

The giant door inched open, making a sound like a hung over elephant stretching in slow motion. I was actually glad the thunder of my heartbeat and wheezy gasps heaving from my mouth helped muffle it.

"Ah, good day to you, mister Radshaw," said the butler in a tone so cheery it made me want to punch his lights out. "I am impressed. I owe Ornias fifty pounds - I bet him you wouldn't make it."

I blinked at him, unable to muster even the faintest sarcasm. "Any ... more ... insults ... to throw ... at me?"

He smiled - at least, I think he did. I was seeing it through a blur of exhaustion. "The Master did not prepare me any scripts for this eventuality. I do not believe he expected you to make it this far. Do come in and have a cup of tea."

"Cheers." I staggered through the door as he moved back. "How come you didn't get altered by the Angwrath's presence?"

I was sorely glad I'd passed him when he replied, because I didn't want to see the face behind his words. In a voice like a million snakes screaming in a pit of fire, he said, "Do not be fooled, Radshaw. This essence is Barrakor the Vile."

I jumped - so big, he must have seen it, because he chuckled. In the world of evil laughs, it reigned supreme - a sound that actually felt like it was reaching up my dick to yank piss from my bladder. "What the fuck are you - the god of serpents?"

"No." He stepped forward and was the butler again, posh English accent and everything. "Patron Saint of paedophiles. Follow me."

"Why do I ask these things?" I muttered.

The inside of Abaddon's castle looked like St Paul's cathedral - if someone set off a dirty bomb in the nave. Black, oily mist curled in a viscous dance from corners in the intricate stonework and slid from surfaces like evil dry ice. It felt like my footsteps should be echoing around the huge space but instead they were swallowed into nothing.

We got almost to the dais before the butler stopped in his tracks. "Ah, what a shame." He smiled at me over his shoulder. "It seems our tea must wait, Radshaw." His voice took on a little of that snake sound as he laughed. "Wait here - The Master will see you now."

A hundred witty retorts collapsed, knackered, on the way to my tongue. In the end, I just shrugged and let myself slump to the grimy stone floor. *If this is it, I might as well get a moment's rest.* I sniffed and looked up at the dais, watching Barrakor the Vile Butler striding away. Bring on the theatrics.

Thunder shook the ground beneath me and I instantly regretted sitting on the floor. I fully expected the demon of death to explode from the ground or crash from the ceiling in a cacophony of destruction and clouds of debris. Instead, Mr Black strolled from a side door, a supercilious smile spread across his face, and the thunder subsided gently.

Something didn't look quite right in his immaculately-groomed exterior. The smile was a little too fixed and he *flickered* as he walked. He looked almost superimposed on existence like a cheap cgi special effect. We're not talking early Babylon 5 space ships or anything - he was more real than that. More like Robert Patrick's liquid metal villain in Terminator 2. It might have fooled innocent eyes, but to a veteran watcher, he just wasn't up to scratch.

"Show your true form, dude. You might as well. I keep hearing how terrifying it is, but frankly, I'm way past the point of rational fear here. If I faint, it'll be a relief and if I don't then at least you can stop pretending and we can get on with talking about all the terrible things you're going to do to me."

The smile disappeared in favour of a wince as he came to a halt several feet away, looking down at me. "I've been called many things during the great span of my existence, Radshaw. Everything from Abaddon to Death to Lord of Destruction, and quite often 'Oh Fuck, Oh Fuck, What the Fuck is That Fucking Thing?'" He leaned forward. "You're the first to call me 'dude' though. I have to say, it makes me feel a little dirty." His face shifted visibly, the humanity dropping in and out like a wet light bulb. Beneath the facade, something blue and furry lurked.

It might have been hysteria, but I felt a laugh bubbling up through my chest as something clicked in my head. "You don't want to show me your true form, do you?"

"What?" He blinked, feigning ignorance, but I was pretty sure I knew better.

"That terrifying aspect you showed my mate Raffa before cutting him in half - the vision so horrid, it froze him on the spot - you can't do that anymore can you?"

His scowl filled the world. "You should be blubbering for my forgiveness, Radshaw. This world knows better than to seek my anger. I am the all and completeness, the beginning, the end, and the ever."

"You're deeply Snickers, mate. That's what you are."

He roared and his face shifted more than ever. Walls shook and that horrid, inky smoke slid across surfaces.

"What makes you so certain of yourself, human? You know this is your death, that escape is impossible."

"I'd say it's my devil-may-care attitude, but I already know he doesn't."

He roared again, shaking the walls, all the more effective for such a huge sound coming from a normal-sized human frame. I gulped as a heavy bole of dread slipped from my stomach into my guts.

Looking him directly in the eye, I clenched my jaw to stop my voice shaking. "Right now, some people might give you a speech about good and bad, how I'm the former and you the latter."

"There's no good and bad, Radshaw - no evil and divine, no right and wrong. Just two sides, fighting to the end of existence."

I felt my lips pulling into a smile. "Exactly why I wouldn't give that speech. Instead, I'll just tell you you're a loser. I'm sitting here on a suspicious warm sensation with no real plan or clue how I'm going to stop you. I'm so scared, there's a good chance this hell domain or whatever it is doesn't even exist - my mind's pretty untrustworthy right now. Still, I came along. I guess I've come to have a go, because I think I'm hard enough."

"Why?" He looked genuinely baffled. My finger twitched against the gun inside my coat. Was it even worth trying?

I winked at him with a confidence I didn't feel. In fact, it was like a snowflake giving the middle finger salute to the sun, but I like snowflakes - I respect their individuality. "Someone has to, or what's the fucking point? Besides, you're bound to bugger up - that's what your kind do."

"My kind? You mean ancient, primal evil with power you cannot fathom?"

"I mean dickheads." I clambered to my feet but stayed hunched over to hide the fact I was grasping two guns. "Face it - you can't even make your fake nice world right. You created a guy everyone wants to fellate, and then built a BJ limit into his junk - that's cruelty of the highest order. Not exactly in keeping, is it?"

"Ah, so it was Azza who helped you - I suspected as much."

"I guess he's as bored of you as I am." I smiled at him. "That's what happens when you spout the same old boring shit constantly - people stop listening."

His nostrils flared. "And you thought what, exactly - you'd come here and annoy me into submission?" The grey beneath was showing more through his face now and a very human drip of sweat was running down his forehead. "You can't do anything to stop me, human. Any action will risk almost certain death, and humans are slaves to their own mortality. It dictates every facet of your behaviour."

I took a couple of deep breaths, feeling the air soaking into my lungs. Far from calming, it gave me sudden flutters in my stomach, but I was on course now. I held to the idea I'd been forming during our confrontation. One solid concept was core to my hope - the Angwrath trumped everything. That was its point and purpose - the ability to even things out.

I blinked as I matched Abaddon's certain gaze. "You're full of confidence, and I guess the demon of death's going to be, but you're forgetting one thing."

"What?"

"I'm Mike Radshaw. I'm nuttier than a schizophrenic squirrel - and you can't ever trust me to behave." I pulled both guns and levelled them at his face. He actually laughed - deep and loud - which meant either he hadn't thought of what I had, or I was deader than a dodo in Star Trek.

"I knew you were foolish, Radshaw, but I never thought you were a stupid motherfucker."

I shrugged. "Big, menacing evil things can't swear like that - it just feels weird. Haven't you seen Blade Trinity?" I kept my eyes focused on him but I couldn't help noticing my tainted hand. The forearm was now completely black and withered. It looked like an ancient, gnarly tree branch coated in crude oil, my fingers like twigs clutching their weapon.

"Films tell us nothing."

"Some motherfucker," I said, channelling Wesley Snipes, "is always trying to ice-skate uphill." Trusting my instincts, I pulled both triggers, and something magical happened.

He flinched. It was a flutter of a moment's hesitation, faster than betrayal and slimmer than the skin of my teeth. But hope is both slimmer and fleeter than betrayal, and in that instant of doubt, I knew I was right.

The bullets slammed into his chest with puffs of white fluff. No blood spilled, no thunder rolled, and no screams of pain filled the cavernous space. Instead, Mr Black finally disappeared as Abaddon gave up on his human disguise. The man in front of me peeled away, skin flopping to the ground like a discarded cape. Eyeballs and teeth tumbled away in its wake, and there before me was a sight that redefined the concept of 'strange.'

Abaddon was a giant grey teddy bear. Granted, his button eyes were glowing like incandescent hatred and the mouth was packed with needle-like fangs, but cute and furry is cute and furry. Matted grey tufts covered his frame and he actually had stitching in all his joints. The rounded ears on top of his head flapped in an invisible breeze, adding to his general adorability.

I snorted. "And there I was think it was fear that'd make me piss myself. I can see the four horsemen now, riding out to strike fear into the populace - War, Famine, Pestilence and Snuggles."

He took a step forward and the ground rumbled. Oh yeah - did I mention he was twenty feet tall? "I'll tear you limb from limb, Radshaw."

I backed up, smiling up at his teddy bear face. "You fell victim to your own plan, didn't you? You made the Angwrath a beautiful fairyland to corrupt, but you couldn't bring yourself to make your own form good or pretty. Out of vanity, you thought you'd be immune, so you kept your evil aspect - that mass of spikes and terror I caught a glimpse of." I winked. "And your own harbinger turned you into a cute teddy bear."

He took another shuddering step. "I still have more power than you can conceive."

"A being so great, it's looking at the universe like a spot on its hand and farts infinities after eating existences like a tin of baked beans. More than that?"

A ripping sound crunched through the air and I gulped as foot-long black claws emerged from the bear's immense paws. He held them up and wiggled them like jazz-hands. "Enough for this."

Bollocks. Trust me to come up against a teddy bear that also happened to be a grumpy X-man. He lunged at me, claws tearing the atmosphere with blinding speed, so I ran for it, firing a gun over one shoulder as I went. The cracking reports of igniting bullets tore into my ear, numbing my hearing on one side, and powder burn pushed syringes into my cheek. Dull thunks sounded from behind me as my shots struck home, but they were too close for my liking.

"Run, you dickwit," I gasped to myself, but my legs refused to take the advice. My gun clicked empty as I staggered between dark pews, muscles quivering and legs juddering with every step. The climb up all those stairs was still taking its toll, along with a fitness level lower than a limbo-dancing gutter snake. I tried to switch hands so I could use the gun I took from the witless security guard, but Mr Black had other plans.

Something slammed into my back with terrible force. For a moment, I thought he'd kicked me, but then I saw the black claws protruding from the front of my chest. I just had time to think, '*great - impaled by a demon teddy bear,*' before he flung me into the air. The claws tore from me as I pin-wheeled towards the ceiling, dragging with them a scream that sounded more like a wheeze. I watched a complex web of my own blood dance in twisting patterns in my wake. It might have been beautiful if I wasn't more worried about landing.

Sure enough, it hurt like a bastard. Turns out, ancient timber pews don't make the best crash-mats. In any decent action film, they'd have crumbled into splinters as I hit them, forming a cushion of debris. Unfortunately, real life - even when you're occupying a version of hell - isn't nearly so considerate. My spine impacted one solid back and I felt my body wrapped the wrong way round its shape. I flopped and rolled, crashing to the foot-well on my face, dragging in one-sided breaths through a throat full of blood. I tried to roll over but pain struck through me, head to foot, so deep and sharp my muscles turned to custard. Tears of frustration bubbled from my eyes and I groaned - it felt like all I could do.

The pews around me were kicked away in a storm of splinters. Huge furry feet settled either side of my shivering form like the pillars of death's gateway. I coughed a thick spatter of clotted blood and phlegm onto the grimy stone floor and tried to move again, this time suppressing the groan out of sheer stubbornness. Abaddon laughed, low and dark, and it sounded like the death knell of hope.

Fuck you.

He was right, I decided as I forced myself to roll over, ignoring the gurgling roar tearing across the back of my throat. There wasn't good or bad, or right and wrong, only sides and players, battling to eternity. This wasn't my eternity - not until I said it was. I came here to do a job, and stupid, scary teddy bear or not, there was one immutable fact burning like a lodestone of determination in my brain:

I wasn't finished yet.

I cast around me, but my guns were gone. The giant teddy leaned over my prostrate form, greasy clumps of stuffing sprouting from him like demonic cauliflower florets where my bullets landed. Its mouth, outlined by stitches, split apart to bare those needle fangs and it laughed again - confident, mocking and victorious.

With every pulse of his rancid breath across my face, my black arm throbbed. It must have been the Angwrath's power that changed it, just like it deadened the landscape outside in an ever-expanding radius and turned Abaddon into a cuddly toy. The arm was my greatest tool against demonic powers - the thing that let me banish them. Much as I hated thinking in those terms, it was my weapon for good. Had it been converted? *Fight fire with fire.* Could it really be so simple?

My foe - Mr Black, The Demon of Death, Abaddon - dropped to one massive knee and planted a paw beside my head, leaning until his flaming button eyes were just inches from my face. "You can't beat me, Radshaw - you never could. Death is everything, the inevitable end and the ultimate arbiter. I am all the things you cannot escape, the fingers that pinch out your last vestiges of hope. Face it, human - it's death that dictates your existence."

"No," I said, the word carried on a breath full of

all the awful memories leading me here. "It's anger."

I slammed my twig-like fist into his hideous mouth, feeling the teeth give way as my hand sank into the soft maw beyond. Where my blackened skin touched, I felt the fluffy matter altering. Dry became wet, softness changing into combinations of slippery rubber and solid slabs. A realisation hit me as he jerked spasmodically, the eyes burning with new fervour. This wasn't a teddy bear head any more. My tainted hand was reverting Abaddon to his original form.

Determination lending clarity to my thoughts and overriding the hideous pain squealing through my chest, I spread my fingers and fisted them again, thrusting my arm back and forth. Bone crunched and splintered, a tongue tried to wrap my forearm but tore away from its base when I flinched, and chunks of gum sluiced from bone as I moved. Then I gripped a handful of pulpy stiffness and realised my hand was in a demon's brain. His body went stiff around my grip and I watched the cute form drop away.

Personality returned to the eyes, along with a horrified expression. A small part of me was laughing hysterically - even ancient demons were repulsed by my touch. Grey fur became glistening carapace, coated in chitinous grooves. Spikes sprouted, hands elongated, and the face turned into a vision of repulsion, dark and exquisitely foul, mouth stretched around the girth of my arm.

Suck it, bitch.

I gripped a mass of splinters and mush with my evil fist, reared both feet up to brace them on his shoulders, and yanked with all my strength. Ignoring the fresh agony ripping through my body, using every ounce of hate and horror at my disposal, I dragged Mr Black's brain and shards of his skull out through his face. His cheeks dissolved and eyeballs pushed sideways to let my fist out in a stringy mess of gore and viscera.

I pushed his convulsing body away to one side with my feet and squeezed the handful of head innards with all my rapidly draining might. Liquefied brain oozed between my fingers, leaving a lace of sinew and gristle woven between my digits, skull fragments caught like flies in a grotesque web. I could feel blood dribbling from my mouth and air rasping through the puckered wounds in my chest. My brain said only one lung was pierced, but the pain sang a mortal song. I needed hospital, and fast, but given I had no easy way back to the normal plane of existence, I didn't see any future ahead.

"Still," I wheezed, "not many people get to say they killed death before kicking the bucket."

"Where did Abby go?" said a boy's voice.

He lost his head. I giggled, uncertain what emotions I was feeling but realising I was completely at their mercy. I looked at the naked boy standing nearby. He was staring at the jerking body of Abaddon and his dishevelled human killer with a completely emotionless expression. He looked about twelve to my inexpert eye. Young and vulnerable and - I hoped - just about pre-pubescent.

I muffled my laughter as I met the Angwrath's gaze. "He's in the place where evil arse-suckers go to die."

"My body might be destroyed, Radshaw, but

here I still abound. Did you really think you'd killed an aspect of darkness and destiny?" The voice came from the walls themselves, throbbing through the air like beats on a bass drum the size of London.

"You won't be threatening anyone in the real world for a while, dickhead. I'll settle for that."

A chugging laugh shook the air. **"I don't need to."** Thunder clapped in the air above the nave, sending a shockwave that tousled my hair and dislodged chunks of masonry. From nowhere, a wind blew up, gale-force and squealing like tortured souls. Before my eyes, a crack appeared in existence. Ten feet high, it floated just above the floor - a black schism - and everything around it looked slightly bent. Another thunderous crash split my ears and the crack widened, exposing a shadowy void behind.

"Go, my child. Return to the place you're destined to alter. Fulfil your destiny and bring about the black dawn."

"No!" I wheezed, but it was barely a sound. The Angwrath nodded and strode into the black slit. I dug deep, plumbing the depths beyond human tolerance, and found a well of strength I hadn't imagined existed. In the face of all hopelessness, knowing my whole life was pointless if I failed, I clambered to my feet, staggered across splinters and bloodstains, and flung myself into the black nothingness of the void.

CHAPTER 8 – BLACK SKY DAWNING

Seething blackness engulfed my senses, riddling my body with electric sensation and crawling across my skin like swarms of ants. I felt myself coughing, wheezing air through the ruptures in my chest and hacking hunks of clotted blood into the ether, but I couldn't hear anything. I knew I was moving because my internal sensors were going haywire, but 'moving' was probably a relative concept when you've just stepped out of hell into a tear through the universe to chase an innocent messiah back to reality.

I studied that last thought for a moment, and then decided it wasn't worth the headache.

Like a sarcastic mosquito caught in a tornado, I span and flipped my way through nothingness. If I'd had anything to throw up, it'd be flying away from me right now in twisting ribbons to coat any onlookers. On the back of that realisation came another - I couldn't actually breathe. Even beyond my deflated lung and the pain gut-punching me from inside with every heartbeat, the frenetic movement meant I couldn't gulp in any air. If this journey took much longer, I'd arrive at my destination a badly dressed, under-deodorised corpse. Lights flashed like LED fireworks in the spaces behind my eyes. I wasn't sure which of the various unpleasant conditions caused them, but at least I had something pretty to look at.

Realising the fatalistic turn my thoughts were taking, I reminded myself why I couldn't die. The Angwrath was trained to be almost entirely bad - that was to say, he'd make everything deeply unpleasant because he'd grown up believing the entirety of existence and its populace was too nice and pretty. Clearly, he'd never watched Jeremy Kyle. He'd bring the black dawn everyone seemed to agree was a bad thing and quite possibly cause the deaths of millions of innocent people.

More importantly, Mister Black did a number on Amy's face. She was the only person worth her salt in the piss-poor experiment called My Life, the only one who made me believe there was anything worth saving about people. She was out of scope, the place bad guys weren't meant to go. If this was a buddy cop action film, she was my 'cop's family' and everyone knows you don't fuck with a cop's family. He broke the rules, and destroying the insides of his head with my magic hand wasn't punishment enough. I had to ruin his plans too. As for the Knights, not only did they let it happen, they actively participated.

Oh yeah, I had some visits to make.

Summoning all my mental strength, which admittedly might have been less than an Atomic Kitten with concussion, I thought about where I needed to be. I pictured the Angwrath - that naked twelve-year-old boy - and did my best not to include his junk in the image. Even in my head, there were some places not worth going. I didn't know how this void travelling thing worked, or where I might get spat out, but if I thought hard enough, believed strongly enough, perhaps-

CRACK!

Air! I wasn't spinning and sweet breath washed into my working lung. The joy might have been greater if I hadn't realised I appeared to be in the sky, falling through thin air. My fear didn't have long to manifest, though - mostly because it turned into fresh pain when my body impacted something smooth, hard, and entirely unforgiving. There were better things to have landed on - a bed of nails perhaps, or a thousand spice girls. Unsure what made me think of that image, I banished it and took in my surroundings.

Under a strangely grey shadow, a broad river snaked into the distance. Not far away was Big Ben or, more precisely, the clock tower that housed it. So, I was in London once more. The realisation might have been more comforting if I wasn't looking *down* on Big Ben. I dragged a shuddering breath and let it ooze out, trying to ignore the hideous agony ripping through my chest. Casting my gaze along the Thames, I saw Charing Cross station and marvelled at how different it looked from the sky.

Finally, something clicked in my brain as the cogs ground away. It was running like an old Celeron without enough RAM *how's THAT for a geeky thought*, but the evidence was clear. I was on the London Eye. I don't mean 'on it' in the sense of taking a ride and snapping some cool piccies. I mean on as in ON TOP. I'd have sighed, but it hurt too much.

My cheek was pressed against the glass of a passenger pod and I could see a thin line of blood trickling away over the horizon of its rounded exterior, drawing a line from my mouth to uncharted territory. Lain flat in the foreground was my arm, somewhat like a fallen tree branch with its bark-like skin and dark colour.

"Gather your wits, Mike." I thought about Trinity

at the start of The Matrix and angled for some of her energy. "Get up, you pussy."

One arm at a time, I lifted myself off the glass. We didn't appear to be in motion and the screams I could hear from below might've had something to do with it. That grey pall was getting darker and a deep chill was emanating from above. Wobbling to my knees, I could see why. Black clouds were descending like alcohol-induced unconsciousness, draping their way across the sky. The sarcastic part of me compared it to a normal London summer but even I had to admit it wasn't usually this bad. *Why in all that's fucked and holy did I reappear here?*

"Why are you foll**owing** me?" demanded a voice from behind. It went from high pitched to death metal growl and back again, giving me a clue who was speaking.

I turned on my knees to see the Angwrath, his feet planted apart and arms held over his head. The first thing I noticed was armpit hair. I know, it's a funny thing to look at first, but we look for what we most fear. With Azza's warnings lurking in my mind, what I most feared was this kid hitting puberty. He was looking at me like a petulant silverback, all power and suspicion. I actually felt the gulp working through my throat. This boy was a human atom bomb on a hair trigger, and that hair was about as stable Kerry Katona on a TV breakfast sofa.

"There are some things you should know," I said, holding my hands up in what I hoped he'd recognise as submission. "You've got your GCSE in Unlimited Power, but you never took the Common Sense module."

He lowered his arms and the dark pall's progress

halted. "Abaddon warned me about you, Radshaw. He said you'd try to confuse me, but I should ignore you."

"He probably also told you he was all-powerful and couldn't be harmed." I shrugged. "Look where that got him." Our eyes met and I could see the raw potential burning behind his gaze, yearning for use. There was just the merest hint of confusion, though. The Angwrath's mould wasn't quite set yet. Like Patrick Swayze in Ghost, I decided the potter's wheel needed my input. "Look around you, kid. Does this look like the world Abaddon brought you up in? He loaded your education, weighted the dice, painted the dominos in his favour. Err, those are metaphors, in case he didn't teach you that."

His chest heaved and I couldn't tell if he was angry, upset or baffled. Mind you, at that age I was usually all three at once.

"I don't have anything else to be," he whispered. "I am the power and the glory, a magnet to all things and beings. Nothing can resist me."

I chuckled. "Yeah, round here we call that the Lynx effect." I shrugged. "But like most advertising, it's really bullshit. In reality, you'll do just as well with a cheap own-brand imitation from Asda."

He blinked. "You speak in riddles, Radshaw. Say what you mean. Why should I not do as Abaddon urged me - what difference is there between life as it is now and the darkness of my bleak oblivion?"

"Probably not a lot, if we get right down to it." I shrugged again, boiling the thoughts down in my head. "But there's one thing here that's more important than anything else."

His eyes burned. "What?"

"Choice."

His nostrils flared visibly as he flexed his underdeveloped body. "This is beyond the whims of man. I serve a purpose for all existence. The choices of humans do not factor."

"Not their choice, not even mine. I mean yours. Listen kid; when a demon you've never met before suddenly gives you a life mission, that's dodgy. He played you by making sure you only saw one very extreme facet of what is. You stand there with your milky white boy-skin approaching the most powerful moment of your life, but dude ... you haven't lived. You talk fancy but there's nothing backing it up."

"What do you mean?"

I looked into eyes as deep as the ocean and yearning like Captain Nemo, and I knew I was right. "You think there's only one path to follow but you don't know *anything*. That isn't choice. That's doing what you're told without question. If what I've heard is right, you're not just meant to appear and kill or bless everything on the spot. You're meant to live here, to understand the way things are so you can know whether there's imbalance."

Shadows rippled like dark water reflections across the pod surface we perched on, playing out a dance of menace and chaos. "I can only be what I am," he whispered eventually.

"And what are you - a disposable camera or the living embodiment of the Big Brother house?" His brow furrowed so I continued quickly. "I don't see a tool that happens to be called an Angwrath. I see a teenage boy with a whole world in front of him - one he wants to explore. Can't you be both things at once?"

His chest was heaving and the glistening in his gaze confirmed his ability to feel. "I don't see a way out of this. The Black Dawn is here to level your playing field."

I glanced up at the roiling clouds. "Crappy weather in London? That's like shitting in a cesspit, kid. Why not put things off? Take some time to live and experience the world. Duplicate some fish or turn the Thames into a cheap Chardonnay. Essex girls'll love that one. Get laid - I hear it's a worthwhile experience."

"My powers are at their peak as I become a man. If I don't act now, they will diminish steadily." His shock of blond hair buffeted in the breeze and, damn it, he looked cute. He wasn't David Beckham struggling for coherency, he was Hugh Grant stammering his way through a romantic approach. "I'll only be able to effect a subtle change."

"Subtle is fine." I took a deep breath and immediately regretted it. "Subtle is meaningful."

We stared at one another for a while as his chest heaved and mine sent waves of nausea through my frame. I was fighting an urgent need to cough. Blood was collecting in my throat, but this felt like a fragile moment and I didn't want to shatter it. The future of the western hemisphere teetered in the balance while one innocent boy wrestled with indecision. Kneeling opposite his anguished expression, probably dying and as spent as Eddie Izzard on his forty third marathon, I couldn't decide if I felt privileged or too exhausted to care. I felt a line trickling from my mouth and my breath piled up against the obstructions in my head.

I sneeze-coughed, leaning forward and gargling out a beautiful combination of blood, bile and phlegm.

At once, the moment was broken. Bare feet thudded towards me and I looked up desperately, realising my head was at exactly the wrong height as the Angwrath stood in front of me. As shadows retreated and the deathly-cold winds subsided, something akin to hope bloomed in my chest. That, or my heart just exploded.

"Thank you, Radshaw. I have much to consider." He planted a hand on my shoulder and pushed me to my back. Agony kicked me in the ribs and I groaned, but it turned to a moan of relief when his bare hand touched my ruptured chest and sweet numbness suffused me. "I think the world needs you in it." His fingers touched my blackened hand and it faded to that subtly grey tint I'd got used to. Still demonic, but no longer looking like a prop from The Mummy. Through the beauty of painless air, I saw him wave a hand awkwardly. "Goodbye."

"Wait," I coughed. "I just want to know one thing." He raised an eyebrow. "Why didn't I change? In Abaddon's domain, my arm turned but the rest of me stayed the same. Everything and everyone was altered except me. Why?"

He smiled. "Not everything needs balance. You're not a good guy, Mike, but you're not a bad one either. Brave or stupid, aggressive or afraid, right or wrong - none of it matters. You're just you." With that, he simply wasn't there. My hair wafted as air rushed to the space he'd vacated.

"Good luck, kid," I muttered as the sun came out, picking detail from London in reflections and shadows. As the maelstrom of madness faded, my ears heard the sirens and shouts from below. I waggled my tongue mentally - this was going to take some explaining.

I rolled to my front and looked down at a gaggle of white-faced tourists in the pod beneath me. Talk about front row seats - and what an angle! I shrugged at them as I shouted through the glass.

"I'd really like to get down now!"

*****

I sat alone in the darkened pub, perched on the single chair I'd dragged into the middle of the floor, and faced the door. After two days of chaos and explaining, I was making a necessary house call. It felt good to be amongst shadows that weren't trying to frighten, maim or kill me. The silence calmed my senses like airborne balm, soaking into my lungs and suffusing my thoughts. The comfortable feeling of my gun holster nestled against my chest wasn't mitigated by the fact it was empty. My jacket pressed the leather into my shirt, against my heart, and it served a purpose.

Presently, keys jangled in the lock, pausing uncertainly - presumably, because the person holding them realised the mechanism was already undone. After a few moments, the door creaked open in a way I could only describe as tentative. A group of guys edged into the common room, squinting at the space before them like asylum seekers emerging from a cargo container. The Knights, afraid of their own lair - how appropriate.

I waited until they turned the light on before smiling. Judging by their expressions, it didn't do much to put them at ease.

"Radshaw..." started the first one - an older guy I didn't recognise.

I held up a hand to cut off what he might say next. "Here's how it is. My level of respect for you guys, whatever it once was, is now lower than an arthritic sloth's speed index. If things turned out differently - if the black dawn was upon us, if Amy died while I was off fixing your fuck-ups ... hell, if I found myself in a slightly worse mood - this place'd be ashes and blood by now. You'd be fighting one another over the remaining intestines to stuff back in the holes where your guts should be."

I pointed to a group of chairs I'd arranged facing my own. "Sit." Their expressions ranged from defiant to meek, but they all complied.

"Now," I fixed each in turn with a stare. "This is how it's going to be. Next time something supernatural's happening in London, you come to me. I'll tell you how it's going to play out, and you'll follow the route I map for you. You don't plot, you don't act, and you don't wipe your worthless arses without consulting me. Understood?" Menace drifted on the air, but I had more than all of them put together. "I'll be taking your silence as total compliance. Five points if you can name the song I just paraphrased." Another silence. "No, I didn't think so."

The old guy who'd first appeared cleared his throat. "So that's it - you just expect us to work for you from now on?"

I shrugged. "I don't expect you to. I know you will. See, you've proved you can't be trusted to do what's best. You followed that dickhead Wilberford way beyond the point of rational consent."

"He's history. We sent him back to the Vatican."

"Too little, too late. The Knights are now my resource, my army to direct as I see fit. I want unfettered access to all your archives, your research materials, the doodles you scribble when you can't sleep at night - and I'm guessing that happens a lot. It all belongs to me."

He shifted again and I decided he was the ringleader. "What do we get in return for this arrangement?"

"You get the warm, fuzzy feeling of knowing you're doing the right thing. You get the reassurance you'll never again try to sacrifice a baby for some fucked up sense of greater good. Most importantly, you get my personal assurance I won't spank you within inches of your lives."

"We work for the Pope." He blew himself up, chest thrust forward. "We are a tool of the most holy."

I almost laughed. "I had to deal with a rancid old gypsy woman to find Mr Black. I gave her my spit, blood and spunk so she could get her jollies, then Black made festival decorations from her innards. I'd walk through hell and drag her disgusting person back into this existence before I defer to your previous master. Fuck the Pope." I pointed at the floor between us. "When he comes here, begs for my forgiveness, and satisfactorily explains why letting Amy get tortured and handing over a toddler to a death demon was the right thing to do ... then he gets a say."

The old guy didn't once look back at his colleagues. His pale green eyes met mine with a calculating gaze. He didn't mind the silence floating between us, and I respected that.

"You're full of shit, Radshaw," piped up someone hiding at the back.

"Shut up, Barnstable," said the old guy, standing up and approaching me with hand extended. "We have a deal Radshaw." I heaved a huge inward sigh of relief as I stood to grip hands with him. "Don't lead us astray. We've had enough of that for all our lifetimes."

I nodded, and then took my leave without another word.

*****

"I just wish I'd been there to see their faces," said Amy, smiling at me from the hideous turquoise pillow of her hospital bed. "With the Knights working under you, you're not going to need an assistant anymore."

I shifted in the chair, harder than a statue of Vinnie Jones and so uncomfortable my arse went to sleep within moments of being placed on it. "Are you kidding? I'll need someone to keep them in line while I'm out getting the shit kicked out of me by terrifying forces of evil."

She giggled and I marvelled at how like herself she looked. Last time I'd seen her, her face looked like squashed steak and kidney pudding. Now, the only trace of all that damage was a network of faint scar lines.

I felt tears filling my eyes. "I never thought I'd be able to look you in the eye again."

"It wasn't your fault, boss. You caught up to him - you sorted him out for me."

"Yeah," I smiled. "I dragged his brains out through his face."

"I feel suitably avenged."

I nodded. "I just can't get over how great you look. I need to send your consultant a fruit basket so big he'll die of health food poisoning."

"I wasn't in a good place." She lowered her eye to avoid my gaze. "It was bad, Mike - there's no denying it. They told me I might not see again, and they'd need to rebuild my face over a few months. But then I went under for the first surgery yesterday and dreamed about a boy. He was naked and happy, and he smiled at me the whole time. When I came round, the nurses were all running round, excited. My face was almost normal - they said it was impossible." She raised her gaze to mine again. "That was him, wasn't it - the Angwrath?"

"Sounds like," I said, nodding. "I'm starting to think this kid might be a messiah worth believing in."

She shifted, wincing. "He's welcome to come back and finish the job."

"Give the kid a break. He's learning to be subtle."

"So, you finally got round to going on the London Eye. Not quite the way you expected, though."

I snorted. "I'm just glad the custody sergeant was

an old mate from my time in The Job. Otherwise, I'd still be in a cell, and they'd still be thinking I was a member of Fathers for Justice. I think I'm going to take a week off."

"No you're not," she chuckled. "Something will go pear-shaped and you'll feel obliged to peel, poach and serve it up for dessert. Besides, I know you're going to look into this Angwrath. It's not every day you meet Jesus' cousin. He's something genuinely new - a force not seen before in modern society."

I nodded. "Well hung, too."

"Mike!"

"What?" I said, grinning. "It was literally two inches from my face - it's not like I tried to notice."

We spent some time in verbal fencing and I settled into the comfort of my friend's company. Life felt alright again. London and I were once more friends, I had a powerful new ally (at least for the moment) and the world was free to flush itself down the shitter.

Until the next time.

The Tall Tale – Part 2

THE TALL TALE – PART 2

As I finished my story, I took another sip of water. It tasted like a thousand dogs took turns to piss in it (don't ask how I know that) but there was no choice -- my throat was in dire need of lubrication.

"You claim much, Radshaw, for one who looks so little." The ginger-haired boy didn't seem so funny anymore. There was something about reliving my recent life that felt incredibly depressing. Perhaps it was all the ball-aching, shit-my-pants terror I'd encountered?

Yeah, that would be it.

"There's more," I said, staring into those soulless young eyes. "I just gave you the highlights."

He snorted and it resounded in the cave-like, fake hospital room. "And yet, I detect no purpose in your coming here. Was it to bore me?"

The funny thing is, I'd actually forgotten my reasons, so caught up was I in telling my tales. There's nothing like telling someone else the things you've done to realise how ridiculous they sound (not to mention *fucking insane*).

"Yes," I said when I saw his brow furrowing. "I decided to face certain death on the off-chance I could threaten a being thousands of years old with the dreaded power of tedium. Seriously, what do you find to amuse yourself for all those years? Do you have any junk left at all?"

The frown slipped away, much to my relief, but he raised his eyebrows instead.

I smiled. "Yes, of course -- my reasons." I did my level best to ignore the sourceless shadow slipping through the air behind Belial's childish form. "Well, I had to make sure I met the boss man."

The shadow coalesced into a humanoid shape, hovering and bobbing behind my captor like a helium-filled sex doll. I made a mental note to mention that analogy later.

The frown was back. "And why, Radshaw," he spat, "would you wish to meet me?"

"Easy." I looked deep into those burning eyes and saw the eternity of pain I'd spend if this all went wrong. The bobbing shadow was turning a fleshy colour. Fleshy with the kind of muscle tone only Hugh Jackman usually pulls off. "I needed to distract you."

The new arrival clamped his arms round Belial from behind, trapping the demon in a musclebound cage. "Are you sure about this, Mister Mike?" said an honest face with eyes of azure gemstones. He had an expression like Channing Tatum on his first date -- quite sweet, really.

Belial roared in anger -- a sound millennia in the making from a tweenage throat -- and I nodded. My ally wrapped one arm round the ginger kid's head and wrenched sharply. A grotesque crunching sound echoed in the room like someone trod on a box of crunchy nut cornflakes. Belial wriggled like mad, kicking and fighting, but then a second wrench turned his face backwards. A sharp crack rang out and he went limp. My saviour grabbed the boy's red hair as he dropped and stood proudly before me, his dead trophy dangling from one fist.

Meet the Angwrath. A child of both angel and demon, begot once every thousand years at the behest of a prophecy as old as myth. He looked about twenty now and it was a good age for him. I'd tried to protect him through his childhood but only barely succeeded in turning him from an evil course. Now, he pretty much did what he wanted -- at my suggestion. I know, I'm a nutter. He carried many names -- Angel's Get, World Shaper, Angwrath -- but these days he preferred Dave.

Right now, though, I had other concerns.

"Seriously, dude," I stared resolutely at his face. "How many times do I have to tell you to put on some fucking clothes?"

He grinned. "You know I don't ever actually put on clothes, Mister Mike. It's all just pretend."

"Well, pretend for me, then. You make me feel like the weedy guy in the Mr Muscle adverts."

In a flash, he was dressed in a white t-shirt and jeans. "Better?"

"Sort of. Even with that top on, your chest looks like a rocky outcrop. Seriously, it isn't fair you get to look like that without the effort."

He waved his free hand and my bonds dissolved away. "Hey, I put in the effort. I go to the gym -- I just slow time down a little so I get ten times the reps. Sure, I could just wish the muscles into place, but where would be the sense of accomplishment?" He shrugged, the dead ginger dancing around in his fist.

I sat up on the solid bed and nodded in the body's direction. "Just so you know, wringing the necks of ten-year-old boys is generally frowned upon. It's not something you should make a habit of."

"What if they really deserve it?" He shrugged huge shoulders. "Can I kill them then?"

I blinked, reminding myself again just how different he was. "Usually, a good hiding is considered sufficient. Otherwise, it's infanticide, and anything bad enough to have a 'cide' named after it should be avoided - you know, as a rule of thumb."

"Well, this one," he said, holding up the dead body, "was demonicide, is that okay?"

I raised my eyebrow at him so he knew I was unimpressed. "Are you sure this will work?"

"I'm still learning too, Mister Mike, but yeah -- I think it should work. We're in his own domain and this was his choice of body. Belial should be trapped in the carcass for a while -- long enough for us to get him somewhere secure. But certain? No, I'm still not sure this is a good idea."

I chuckled. "Nothing I do ever seems like a good idea. But the ancient text is adamant we need a captive essence -- and a powerful one, at that. It's our only chance to avoid oblivion." I blinked. "How come the end of existence sounds so lame?"

"On the last day of life, everything will sound lame."

I gave him a shrewd look. "Philosophy class?"

"Just my upbringing." He smiled. "This dude's getting heavy. Can we leave now?"

"Okay, do your thing. The Knights found a place they say can hold him."

"The Knights say many things without telling much." He looked around the space and mists began to float as though obeying his gaze.

I chuckled. "Yeah. They're like Viagra -- nobody wants to admit needing them, but everyone has a phone number in their back pocket."

The shadows swirled around us, binding our limbs and minds in their embrace, and I looked up at the Angwrath's powerful face. "You know, when you were appearing, you looked like-"

"A sex doll, I know. I can read your thoughts like they're written in the sky, remember?" The misty darkness congealed around us and whisked our shapes into the ever-shifting storm cloud of the ether.

"Ah, Dave," I sighed. "You take all the fun out of life."

BONUS STORIES

The following are much older stories with links to Mike Radshaw and his universe. They are presented in their original forms, complete with some amateurish writing and lots of imagination!

Satan Claws was the first time I used the name, although he's developed a lot since those days. It does provide some background and a little texture around what was to come.

Don't Follow Me Down doesn't feature Mike Radshaw directly, but it's set in the same reality. Our characters are victims of, or at least influenced by, his crazy shenanigans.

SATAN CLAWS

There is a creature. A very old and primal creature. In medieval times his story was whispered in the cold, dark halls of castles at night. Stockings were hung at vulnerable access points, such as fireplaces, packed with cloves and holly berries; said to be his most hated scents. Barbed erections graced every house, both tribute to and warning of his power, bedecked in red-inked lanterns lest any forget his aspect. Knight and peasant alike slept with weapons before wives, praying they would not have to defend their families. Every soul in the land lay awake all night, wishing desperately for the dawn, listening out for hoofbeats on the roof, shaking.

But reality becomes legend, and legend becomes myth. And myths? Well, myths fall victim to the ever-hungry media machine, and before you know it, advertising is supplying us with our reality ...

*****

Jenny trudged down the stairs, a haggard but happy smile gracing her thirty-something face. Her husband Gerald watched her over his shoulder from his perch on the bottom step.

"Are the monsters asleep?" he asked.

"The monsters are in bed," she replied, dropping down next to him on the bottom step, "but sleep? I'm not a miracle worker, and I'm saving the drugs for our next party." Gerald chuckled and put his arm around his wife of six years, hugging her close.

"Remind me to avoid that one; a sleeping pill party might lack something in the energy department."

She snorted into his shoulder. "Okay clever-dick, not my best thought-out joke ever. I'm so knackered right now I'd probably find the Royal Variety Performance funny. And no, that doesn't mean we can put it on, even if it is Christmas Eve."

They moved into the living room and settled down on the sofa together, a bottle of port by their feet and a cheesy old movie on the television.

"Shall we put the stockings up on the mantelpiece again this year?" asked Gerald.

"No, let's just do presents under the tree this time. No opening before we've had Christmas dinner though, or Mum will have a fit."

He sucked in a breath. "You'll have a rebellion on your hands in the morning with that policy. Let them have one each first thing. Your mum with find a reason to have a fit anyway, best not to combine it with grumpy kids."

Jenny chuckled. "Your wisdom is grand, my husband. It shall be as you say."

They laughed together, drank some more port, then arranged presents under the Christmas tree before collapsing into a loving heap together in bed, enjoying their last moments of peace before the Christmas storm.

*****

His heavy exhalation bubbled froth and mucus

between his distended teeth, then sucked the thick mixture back in when it breathed once more. His name was Nic, and he surveyed the dark world arrayed below as he galloped across the night, riding a fel Reign on loan from Hell. Black-red skin glistened with the moon's reflection, sliding between the shadows of the Eve sky like a black velvet comet. His hugely muscled chest prevented him from looking human, and his tiny, pencil-like limbs were grotesquely inappropriate for his size. He looked and studied, searching for an unprotected entrance, and finding one was not difficult.

An inviting chimney loomed out of the gloom. A growl in the ear of the Reign, and they were descending. As its hooves clanked onto roof tiles, cracking them with heat, the Reign snorted and tossed its head, flaming antlers whooshing. Nic kicked the goat-like animal brutally in the stomach with a hanging heel, and growled again, spattering the hellspawn with snot and bile. Then he dismounted onto legs that should not have been able to carry him.

As he stood proud, his silhouette revealed his defining feature; a huge, barbed phallus, inches thick at the base, extending two feet long and crowned with a thorned star, its entire length swathed in barnacles and claw-shaped extensions. As his arousal grew, a coughing gurgle shunted from his mouth in sprays of phlegm. *Yo-ho-ho, yo-ho-ho*

With a final warning growl at the Reign, he grasped a chimney pot, and vaulted into the opening, his distended body wedging hard, then seeming to morph and elongate as he crunched and ground his way into the chimney. The metal fireplace at the bottom bent almost flat as he landed on it. He pulled himself fully erect in the living room, until his ears brushed the ceiling. The tree by the window made him chuckle, and he threw it a glib salute. A drink and a pie caught his eyes, sat on a small plate on the mantelpiece. The drink had alcohol, so he devoured it for fuel, the glass crunching pleasantly in his mouth. Then the sweet odour of a female caught his nostrils, flaring them like trumpets. He grumbled softly in pleasure, ichor sticking to his chin, foam billowing and contracting around his mouth as his breathing accelerated. *Yo-ho-ho*

The stairs squealed in complaint as he mounted them, boards cracking and nails bending. Small hissing sounds issued as his phallus dripped acidic juice on the carpet, a product of his burgeoning excitement. He needed satisfaction. It had been too long in coming, and this would be a sweet release.

He reached the landing, and two small humans ran into view from a side door. He batted them aside contemptuously, eager now for his prize, and pounded toward the far door. Its weight was nothing to his blow, and through a cloud of splinters he saw a human male swinging a bat towards him. It bounced from his skull, tickling him slightly, then the look of shock on the humans face was comical. Nic reached forward, grabbed the face, and plucked it from the man's skull, then kicked him into a corner.

A woman's scream rent the air, and Nic's excitement peaked so sharply he almost climaxed. He clambered onto the bed with the screaming figure, crushing its legs with his weight. He grabbed her, flipped her over, and pushed his phallus eagerly into her. As he drew out, then rammed his hips forward again, her screams became choking coughs, then gurgles and moans. His climax came in a stuttering, bursting collection of releases. *Yo ... ho ... ho ... Yo-ho-ho. Yo-ho-ho*

*****

Detective Mike Radshaw sat outside the Intensive Therapy Unit, tapping his toe. Two in the morning his phone had woken him, a very pissed-off sergeant demanding he get to the hospital. *Merry Christmas to you too, Sir.* He checked his watch. Two thirty. Not bad going, but traffic had been non-existent as no other bugger was foolish enough to be out. He'd left a house consumed with emptiness, the ghosts of a family many-years faded his only companions. *Fuck it. Who needs Christmas anyway?*

The door behind him opened, and a pasty-white young PC walked out on wobbly legs. Mike stood and walked over.

"How's she doing?" The PC looked at him with eyes not seeming to comprehend the question, then laughed. Mike steered him to the chairs and sat him down. "Come on, son, focus. Pull yourself together! What does it look like?" The young man barked a laugh with no humour.

"LOOK LIKE? It looks like she was arse-raped by a barbed wire Christmas tree!" The man laughed again, a near-hysterical yelp with an eerie edge.

"What about the husband, and the kids?" persisted Mike. The PC seemed to calm a little.

"The husband died of shock shortly after arrival. The boy was dead at the scene, the girl's in ITU with her mother. Her back is broken."

"Alright. Go get a coffee, son. You have the address? Thanks."

*****

The stairs in the family's house looked like an elephant had used them, but they took Mike's weight as he ascended. The irregular round burn-holes in the carpet were giving off an odour like fresh-cut grass, mixed with burnt hair. On the landing the blood spatters started, and when he reached the bedroom at the end of the upper hall, there were no more spatters. There were pools. The darkness seemed to close in around him, and he started to wonder why he didn't call for backup, and more so why he hadn't turned a light on.

Then a soft voice behind him almost made him faint.

"We call him Nic. A name with many connotations."

"What the FUCK!" shouted Mike, spinning and backing up.

"Calm down detective, I'm just an old man." A face loomed out of the darkness. Sure enough, an old face, lined but firm, it's thin white beard complementing a serious and hardy face. "I'm not here to threaten you."

"I almost shit my pants! Who are you, and what

are you doing in here? This is a crime scene." More to the point, he wondered, why wasn't he putting the old guy in an arm-lock and frog-marching him off the premises? There was something ... trustworthy about the old codger.

"You'll have to trust me, detective, as we have no time for explanations beyond the most profoundly simple. This was not a human crime. Your perpetrator is an ancient Daemon, one of the oldest of the Fae. We call him Nic, though medieval humans had a more primal name for him; Satan Claws. You can consider the ramifications later."

Mike shook his head, trying to remove the wooziness this man caused. "You are having a giraffe with me, aren't you mate?"

"I used to take offence to your kind of idiocy. Nowadays it just bores me."

"Thanks."

"Just listen," said the old man, his voice now sounding testy. "Nic is about seven feet tall. He looks like Arnold Schwarzenegger with a toddler's limbs. He's all dark red of skin, he'll be naked, and you wont be able to miss the two-foot-long phallus that's sticking out of the front of him. He'll have froth bubbling around his neck, waist, and cuffs from the exertion of keeping himself in our plane. He's not far, and I need your help to stop him."

Mike almost laughed. "I'm sure I don't remember doing any drugs. There's a demon in my town, raping women with a spiky cock, and you're here to fight him, but you need my help? Have I been transported into a straight-to-DVD horror film?"

"You haven't, yes, and no, to answer those questions." The old man sighed. "I am a knight, and far older than I look. No quips please. I've been fighting creatures like Nic my whole life. He can only be stopped by the removal of his phallus. That will slow him down for a few years at least, until it grows back, and more importantly will shock him back to the Daemon plane."

"So hang on," Mike said, keeping his face straight, still certain he was tripping or dreaming. "You want me to come with you so I can chop off a demon's cock to stop him fucking any more women. Do I have that right?"

"No, detective. I'll chop off his cock. I need you to distract him."

*****

"I thought you were fucking pulling my leg!" whispered Mike. He was peeping around a corner into a back-alley, the old knight crouched behind him. He felt a little more normal now, although he still trusted this stranger completely. His mind seemed to have decided to simply go along with things.

"I don't pull legs," replied the knight.

Nic, Satan Claws, whatever his name may be, was hunched over a weakly struggling tramp in the alley, his hand fastened to her wrist. He seemed to be waiting for something.

"When do we go for him?" asked Mike.

The knight's face was deadly serious as he replied, "when he is at his most distracted."

A scream dragged Mike's attention back to the scene before him, and as the creature shoved the struggling woman to her face and reared up, Mike saw for the first time that huge, glistening, spiked phallus. *Like a barbed wire Christmas tree...*

His instincts roared in protest on the most primal of levels. "Get that thing away from her!" he yelled, hurling himself into the alley towards Nic. The daemon snuffled in surprise, and turned its head to face him, a face that was all teeth at mad angles, and an array of eyes across the brow. Anger burned in that horrific face. Nic kicked his victim to stop her running, and turned to face Mike, throwing his arms wide.

Mike stopped, and pulled his gun from its shoulder holster. He didn't know why he wasn't frightened, but he was going to take full advantage. He faced off against the abomination, and settled into a firing stance. Satan Claws roared, spewing phlegm and filth from his mouth.

"You're one ugly motherfucker!" said Mike, and emptied his automatic into the face. Another roar, and from the side came an old man, glowing with white light, the barest hint of wings behind him. He swung a shining arm, and a bloodied, two-foot-tall Christmas tree tumbled through the air. A scream sounded, and Mike's senses overloaded.

*****

Detective Mike Radshaw laughed at his father's terrible joke, and pulled his mother's cracker. Tired from a presumably restless night, he nevertheless felt happy for no reason other than that he was with his family, and that was enough. There was some news on the telly about a family who'd been attacked in the night, but the mother and daughter had turned out to be less badly injured than first feared, and would make a full recovery. Mike couldn't shake the feeling that something momentous had happened, but for now he wouldn't worry. For now he'd just enjoy Christmas.

Don't Follow Me Down

"You mustn't go in there, Simon. Ppp-" the faintest of coughs shook her frame, rattling in her frail throat. Blood oozed from the corner of her desperate smile with a wet, slick sound. A shallow breath wheezed. "Promisssss." Her voice trailed off in time to a bloodshot tear that crawled down her temple into the hair tangled on the dank ground like a discarded mop.

"I don't understand," I whispered. "What's in there? What did it do to you?"

She gazed into my eyes. "You look red, my love," she whispered. "Everything looks red. Is there blood in my eyes?"

My furious breaths burned my throat. It was a wonder she could see at all. Blood wasn't so much in her eyes as everywhere; her bed, blanket and make-up. *If only I'd got here sooner!* I squeezed my eyes shut so hard it hurt my brain, willing away this horrid reality, but I knew it was a hopeless wish.

"A little," I answered. "I have to get you out of here. I'll carry you to hospital, I don't care how far. I don't want to lose you!"

Her hand brushed weakly at mine. "If wants had power we'd all be angels, Simon, strumming our harps till kingdom come. This is my fault; I did this. Now let me be. It's almost time, I can feel the life draining out of me."

I knelt on the grimy stone, my hands shaking as frustration riddled my system. "Let me try. I have to try."

She smiled again, a watercolour dream of her

usual beaming grin. "I think the back of my head's missing. If you lift me ..." Her voice trailed off but I got the picture. A shadow of fear crossed her face then. "Simon. SIMON?" She coughed a fine crimson mist across my face but I refused to close my eyes.

"I'm here, my love." Even through the blood I could see the glaze in her eyes and something repulsively heavy settled in my gut.

"I can't see you," she mumbled, the last word sputtering, her mouth the only animated part of her face. Then she was still.

I watched as my tears fell away in my vision and collected in the dead wells of her face. My knees were soaked with her blood and the mess her head rested on lent weight to her earlier assessment. Her hair spread like crimson snakes from her head. Medusa, realised in gore.

I stood and gazed through blurry vision at the door she'd gone through, now closed without explanation after her escape. It shimmered slightly, even in the gloom of the tunnel, as though I was viewing it through a heat haze. It seemed hewn from a single slab of ancient timber, knotted and creased. Scrawled across it were runes of some kind, spidery and sinister.

I looked down at the love of my life, her ravaged form a sickening rictus on the ground. I let the image soak into my mind, scribed forever into the tablet of my memory by horror and anger.

"I will return," I whispered, my hands clenching until my fingernails pierced my palms, "and I will avenge you, my Sophie."

*****

Dear Brenda and John,

I am so sorry. Your daughter, my beloved Sophie, is dead. I was too late, you see. She had foolishly plunged into the darkness and returned before I got to her. The damage to her head was too great, and I was helpless to save her.

If I have disappeared when you read this, please do not look for me. I must follow where she went. I must understand what killed my Sophie. If that means descending to the depths she sought, then so be it.

I hope you do not bear me any ill will.

See you sometime, soon I hope.

Simon

*****

The pain stabbed into me as I prepared to follow Sophie, spreading through my system with its poisonous promises. It was assuaged by my certainty that this had to be done. I needed to know what had happened to her. I had to face her demons. The world swam before my eyes but my grief and anger kept me buoyant.

Before long I stood before that door. I realised then why it seemed familiar. I'd read the description before, in a newspaper article. Some mad ex-policeman called Mike Radshaw had been posting adverts for 'warriors' to help him solve the mystery of strange doors that he'd been encountering. He'd caught the attention of the press and they'd written a tongue-in-cheek article, but Mike hadn't been tongue-in-cheek at all when he described these doors. He'd been outright scary, and deadly serious.

I grasped the handle, pulled the portal open, and stepped into an existence of utter black. A chill wind wafted against my face, carrying an odour like dead animals in a dustbin. I staggered forward, hands outstretched, determined to continue. I heard a low groan off to one side and almost jumped out of my skin. I had thought I was in a tunnel of some kind, but apparently that wasn't so. A moan slipped through the darkness from the other direction and suddenly I wanted to be able to see very much. Beads of sweat were tickling my forehead and driving lines of ants down behind my ears. Then a whisper floated to me in the breeze.

"Come to us," it called in a multi-layered susurrus. My bladder almost gave way on the spot and I could feel the fear pushing through my insides like greasy hands, grasping at my organs with merciless pressure. I staggered a little and put an arm out for balance, but there was nothing to shore me up and I crashed to my knees.

A deep, primal mumbling was coming from somewhere nearby, the voice tinged with hopelessness and drenched in loss. I couldn't make out the words, but the monotonous grumbling grated against my senses and wrenched at my heart.

"I'm sorry," I said, tears tracking my face. "I'm

sorry I couldn't save you, my Sophie, but I can avenge you."

A sibilant hissing issued from just in front of me and I whimpered. A rattlesnake's laugh rolled across my consciousness.

"Vengeaaaaannnnnnnccccccccce," whispered the hiss, laughter gifting it a sense of blackest dread. "No vengeanccccce, only feeeeaaaaar."

The sight of Sophie came to me then, dead in repose, crimson snakes spreading from her mind. My resolve hardened once more and I clenched my jaw. "I would face you," I said with as much conviction as I could muster. I pushed myself to my feet once again, fighting the shakes that stammered through my frame. "Show yourself."

The soft laughter came again, filling my senses with malice, and I was very aware that I was way out of my depth. I was the impostor here, invading enemy territory with only grief and hate to back me up. They would have to be enough.

Light blossomed as a fire sprang to life before me, as red as Satan's eyes and as hot as Hell's passion. It seemed to emanate from the floor itself. As it grew, before my eyes a deeply feminine silhouette was revealed. Her curves were perfect dreams, her body clearly naked even in outline. Atop her head were dancing snakes, the mark of the mythical Gorgon. The difference was that the flailing ends were tails, the snakes' heads buried deep inside her head. As the fey light brightened further, I took a step back in shock. The Gorgon was Sophie.

"No!" I shouted. "You are not her!"

The laughter issued again between sharpened fangs and peeled back lips as she danced, swaying sensuously to a rhythm all her own, a motion perfectly judged to accentuate her nudity.

"Oh, but I am her. The other her, the better her, the her who deserves to be the only one."

I stepped forward, my anger giving me courage. "You are a sick likeness, a demon, a nether creature! You are not her, and you do not deserve her image."

Slitted eyes met mine, sharp with malevolent fervour. "She does not need the form any more. It is mine now, torn from her in fairness, ripped from her uncaring grasp."

I stepped closer. "I should kill you." I pulled my flick knife from my pocket and sprang the blade. "You left her damaged and alone, her life spilling from her form."

She began to circle and I turned with her, keeping her grotesque image in front of me. Her laughter had ceased and those evil eyes looked deadly serious. "She did it to herself, little boy. Do not replicate her mistake," she hissed.

I leapt forward and plunged my knife into her neck. Instead of trying to stop me, she let me come, and my stomach turned at the sensation running up my hand as my blade parted flesh, sinew and muscle. There was no blood, only an increasing limpness in her form. She looked into my face, our noses touching as the dancing light outlined her features in orange. Those beautiful, familiar features, made alien by this terrible place. Then she kissed me, just the once, and laughed mockingly through her death rattle.

A tear escaped my eye as I held her upright form. "What have I done?" I whispered.

Then pain speared into me from behind, stinging me sharply and repeatedly. It felt like a succession of bites... snake bites! There was another figure behind me, and the hissing of serpents filled my ears. My knees buckled as pain tore through my joints. I felt like my bones had turned to acid and melted my muscles. I collapsed to the floor and writhed, catching a glimpse of a naked male shape with snakes instead of hair. This time, the snakes faced outward and I wondered why.

I looked up into the grinning face and knew a sensation of total betrayal. My killer, my victor, my vanquisher, laughed an insane cackle. As darkness pulsed at the edges of my vision and the fire's heat was lost to me, I roared with anguish and sobbed like the baby I wished to be.

My betrayer, my defeat, was me.

*****

"He's just up here, through this door," said Officer Harris. "Are you sure you want to see this?"

Brenda and John both nodded. "His parents died when he was young," said John, pulling his jacket tight against the cold. "We feel kind of responsible for the lad. He would have been our son-in-law soon enough."

Harris nodded as they walked along the filthy alleyway. "You know he was into this shit?"

Brenda whimpered slightly, tears staining her face. "Our daughter bit the apple some time ago, we hoped Simon wouldn't follow her."

They followed Officer Harris through a flimsy metal door into a scene from a dark nightmare. Stained blankets littered the concrete floor of a hollowed-out building. In the centre of the room, a hole had been dug in the concrete, apparently for use as a fire pit. The police had set up flood lights around the place and small, bearded people huddled in the shadows, guarded by more police. One of the homeless guys was mumbling incessantly in a droll, monotonous voice, and several others moaned softly. Next to the fire pit was a body, spread in an arrangement of pain.

"Oh, Simon," whispered Brenda as they approached.

John nodded. "Poor, stupid bastard."

Simon lay twisted on the ground, as though he'd died writhing. Foam flecked his lips and dribbled down one cheek onto his neck. Blood had dried in streaks across his face and stained deep blotches in his trousers. One arm was bound tight with a length of rubber tubing. The inner elbow sported a half-pressed syringe, pulling a tent of skin where it hung from his vein. The whole lower arm had turned a dark grey colour.

Officer Harris sighed. "It was a heart attack that killed him, caused by a huge drug-fuelled increase in his blood pressure. The attack was so big and sudden it ruptured his system, and he bled out from every orifice on his body."

"He said he was going after her," John mumbled, "that he wanted to face what killed her. I wonder what he saw, what twisted visions led him on?"

Brenda sniffed. "I hope he found peace. Do you think he found peace? John, do you?"

John gazed down at the dead young man at his feet.

"No," he said. "I don't."

ABOUT THE AUTHOR

Michael E Bell was born in 1976 on planet Earth, and usually he likes to live there. He cut his teeth on poetry at the tender age of eight, and spent his school years looking for the narrative behind lesson plans.

Now he spends his days keeping up with all the stories backed up in his head, trying to write them before they defect in search of a less barmy outlet. Sometimes, you see, the words want to play, and woe betide he who ignores them.

WANT TO KNOW MORE?

If you'd like to be informed of new releases by Michael E Bell and news about upcoming adventures, please check out the Michael E Bell facebook page:

https://www.facebook.com/authormichaelebell

Bran's Torment

Can a bitter young man, filled with hatred, halt an ancient conflict and bring peace to the lands?

Bran is a military courier with a painful past and a head full of hatred for the blue creatures the people call 'goblins'. All he wants is to do his job and help humanity drive away the goblin threat, preferably in as violent a manner as possible. Fate, however, has other plans. Bran will become the focal point of a historic conflict that goes back further than he can imagine. To succeed, he must learn to trust others, conquer his fears, and face the horrors of his past.

His story follows him through pain, friendships, love, and the biggest battle in living memory, ultimately arriving at his self discovery - a revelation that will irrevocably alter the politics and populace of the known world.

Onekka
The Tragedy of Jaqui Fennet

***In the endless night of space,
reality is not what it seems.***

The world's first viable off-world community, Onekka is a technical marvel - a space station that showcases the best in human achievement, a platform for research and development in the ultimate sterile environment.

Jaqui Fennet has lived there since the station's inception, and played a key part in its growth. She knows Onekka like a mother knows her child, proud of every achievement. Or does she?

When a strange disappearance leads Jaqui to question the innocence of her baby, reality starts to unravel. Each question she asks deepens her predicament, and soon she finds herself lost between the sudden violence of the present and a past she tried to forget. Strange voices accost her dreams with prophetic predictions, agents and investigators dog her heels, and nobody in her life seems trustworthy.

In the end, Jaqui will be faced with two distinct possibilities: Is she going insane, or has she stumbled upon the biggest conspiracy in the history of the Earth?

Onekka is a novel about what it means to be human, and whether understanding that is the key to enlightenment or oblivion.

Free Man's Game

How far would you go to uncover the truth?

Journalist Nick Hubris wants a real story - something that doesn't involve a drunk footballer or kinky politician. What he finds is something so fundamentally incredible that no editor in their right mind will publish it.

One strange event will set him on a path of confusion, kidnap, revelation and violence that just might win him a Pulitzer - if he can avoid getting shot in the process.

Free Man's Game is a novella about getting in too deep, and consequences beyond imagination.

The Chronicles of the Wandering Man

When the world is reduced to nothing, what happens next?

The Wandering Man strides through a world of abject desolation, all civilisation a hundred years dead. Kept alive by mutation and a burning desire to understand what happened, he seeks a purpose; a destiny that's worth fulfilling.

The Chronicles of the Wandering Man is a narrative poem that asks us how far we might go, how determined we might be, in the face of a battle where all the stakes are irrelevant, and everything worth fighting for has already been lost.

Winner of the prestigious Fanstory.com Seal of Quality award.

e

—